QUAKE

Books by Rudolph Wurlitzer

NOG
FLATS
QUAKE

QUAKE

A novel by Rudolph Wurlitzer

E. P. Dutton & Co., Inc. | New York | 1972

Published simultaneously in Canada
by Clarke, Irwin & Company Limited, Toronto and Vancouver

SBN: 0-525-18660-3
Library of Congress Catalog Card Number: 72-82696

QUAKE

I was thrown out of bed. The mirror fell off the wall and shattered over the dresser. The floor moved again and the ceiling sagged towards me.

It was dawn and I was in the Tropicana Motel in Los Angeles. There was another trembling through the room and what sounded like wires snapping and windows breaking. Then it was very quiet. I lay back on the floor and shut my eyes. I was in no hurry. There was a high prolonged scream by the pool and then a splash and another, shorter scream. I stood up and raised my arms over my head and tried to touch my toes, an early morning ritual I never perform. The wall next to the bed was moving as if it was alive and I walked into the bathroom.

I sat down on the edge of the bathtub. The door banged open in the other room and a lamp crashed to the floor. A small man in black silk jockey shorts crawled towards me. His black hair was parted in the middle and there was an oblong birthmark the size of an ostrich egg on his left shoulder. He managed to crawl to the doorsill of the bathroom before he collapsed. After a long moan, he began to cry.

"The ceiling fell in on me," he whispered. "My hips are crushed. My leg is broken and something bad is happening inside. You got to help me."

He propped himself up by the door, his eyes full of rage and shock.

"I'm room six," he said. "Next door. The phones are out. It's going very fast. I figure it for an earthquake. I'm scared, man. It's going altogether too fast."

Blood was forming on one side of his mouth. His head tilted back. Then he threw up in short violent spasms. When he was finished he wiped his mouth on the back of his wrist and looked up at me again.

"It's going to be a long day. But if we're not dead now we probably won't be. I'm hemorrhaging or something. I'll wait here. But don't forget me. You forget me and I'll come after you. Everything is in my wallet. Room six. I got credit cards."

He sank down to the floor and put his arms over his head. He had curled in on himself like a baby. He was very still. I knelt down beside him. He was dead. I stepped over him and walked to the bed. I couldn't find my pants and I pulled off a sheet and twisted it around me. Then I went outside. There were no lights on and I could hear the dial from a portable radio being twisted quickly from station to station. The cabins were arranged on two landings around three sides of the kidney-shaped pool. The open side faced Santa Monica Boulevard where a broken water main squirted a stream twenty feet in the air and a telephone pole swayed forward, as if about to fall across the length of the street. The cabins were a faded blue and white and the brown plywood doors were chipped and smudged from banging suitcases and prodding boots, the law and otherwise. It was a reasonably priced, almost cheap motel, plastic and transient. Except for me. I was becoming known as a regular. I had fallen in three months ago from New York and was waiting for my money to run out. Then I would either borrow more or cop some and take a ride somewhere else, San Francisco or Vegas, it didn't matter. I wasn't above panhandling, spiritual or otherwise, movie extra, weekend carpentry or genteel smuggling. But New York was different than L.A. It had taken time for me to get it together, to get used to a different set of rituals and corruptions. But all that didn't matter right then. I walked over to the diving board on the cabin side of the pool and crawled out to the end. I wanted to sit on the most precarious space available, as if to prove to myself that the event was already over. No one was around except for a body across the pool huddled beneath a bath towel on a yellow chaise lounge. It was suddenly very peaceful, as if the earth had never trembled at all. I lay on my stomach over the length of the board, my arms hanging over the water.

A foot rubbed against my ankle at the end of

the board. "Either let me in or give me the fucking key."

I looked up at her torn white sneakers with one pink toenail visible and then at her faded blue jeans. Two inches of her round stomach was exposed between her belt and pale orange tee shirt.

"You're not Jerry," she said. "I thought you was Jerry."

I twisted around to face her. A few feet behind and to the left of her a barefooted fat man in cuffed brown slacks and white undershirt took two steps out of cabin seven, then a quick third, and considered the dawn. A small haggard woman in curlers and an open blue dressing gown that exposed one deflated breast stepped slowly after him. She was crying and scratching her hip with one hand and trying to put the other arm around him. He shrugged her off, preferring to fold his arms across his sagging chest and swing his head back and forth like it was loose on its pivot. The girl on the diving board kicked my leg.

"You look like you're in shock," she said. And then again. "You look like you're in shock."

I looked up at her. Her heavy breasts more than filled her tee shirt and her neck was short and crouched between her shoulders like she was about to snap. Her features were arranged in a strangely geometric order, a kind of precise oasis between her wild brown curls sticking straight out from her unusually small head. She was around eighteen.

"Did the ceiling fall in on you?" She prodded

at my foot. I began to suspect that she was not altogether in control.

"I got out all right," I said. "Nothing happened."

She stepped back and stared off across the pool, her arms folded across her breasts. She seemed unable to move one way or the other. A young man in a brown and gold flecked business suit, without shirt or shoes, stepped briskly out of cabin twelve. He cupped his hands around his milk white face and shouted across the pool.

"7.6 on the Richter scale and you should get off the diving board. Did you hear what I said? 7.6 on the Richter scale."

He walked off to the side of us and stood near the office. The girl dropped her arms and then slowly raised one hand and gave him a slowly rotating finger. He stared open mouthed at her, the back of his wrists braced girlishly on his hips. Two stout, white haired women rushed out of cabin twenty-three and leaned over the iron railing above him. The one on the left wore blue hot pants, the one on the right a rose patterned black and white mu-mu. The one with the hot pants leaned further over the railing.

"Did you say 6.5?" Her voice started as a yell but broke into a whimper. The other woman slapped her across the face and then slapped her again. The man in the brown and gold flecked business suit stepped out a little and looked up at them.

"7.6," he yelled. "The whole San Fernando Valley might go. They got a dam out there and if the pressure builds up any more you can forget about it."

The girl sat down cross-legged on the diving board. It was an awkward position for her but she seemed determined to hold it.

"Fuck them," she said. "Pressure. What do they know about pressure? I don't care if the whole state goes. I'm up to here. All I can think about is the goldfish falling out of all the tanks. There must be eight million goldfish in this town."

I wasn't watching myself, so to speak, but the action around the pool. Somehow I felt a need to delay my own reaction as long as possible.

The manager of the motel stumbled out of the office. He was old and white haired and wore baggy yellow flannel pajamas. He walked around the pool with his eyes to the cement, checking for cracks. When he had returned to the office he stopped and shaded his eyes towards Santa Monica Boulevard. He stood that way for a long time before he opened the door and disappeared.

"I came back late," the girl said. "You don't mind if I talk like this, do you? You're not doing anything, are you? I'm not going to be able to talk much longer. I can feel it. This is my rush now. They were all fucking around inside with their video tapes and dope and experiments in some kind of science. They're English. Room eighteen. You don't mind, do you? All they do is play music and put everything down. Snort coke, bitch about the air conditioning, watch the tube. It's a life. Their group makes bread. You don't mind if I go on like this? Well, shit, I'm from Montana. Northern Montana. I don't need them. Heh heh. I was sitting out here and the water hit me and woke me up. I was scared. I was so crazy I ran around and tried to scoop the water back into the pool. Talk it back, you know. I been here three days. Four days counting today. I might go to London. They have a house in London. I never been anywhere except for three weeks in London. I mean Denver."

She stared off across the pool. There was a slight tremor and she dug her nails into the bottom of my foot. I screamed.

"Is it?" she yelled. "Well, is it? This is it, isn't it? But they have these all the time out here, don't they? They got some kind of a fault underneath. Don't they? You can answer me. It's all right. Don't do a number on me. OK? It's passed. I think it's passed."

"What do you care?" I pushed her back with my foot. My voice sounded very loud to me. "So what if it comes down? Who are you to choose sides? You can't go anywhere. You're totally lamed out as it is."

She shrugged. "Yeah, you're right."

I watched the side of the pool.

The form underneath the bath towel slowly stretched and the towel dropped over the back of the plastic chaise lounge. A massive and leonine head

13

appeared, with golden curls swirling over narrow pinched shoulders. A full blond beard covered most of the granite shaped face but the eyes, even from the diving board, were an electric pink and piercing blue.

"I seen him around," the girl said vaguely. She watched me anxiously. "He plays base guitar somewhere and knows about mushrooms and Kundalini."

His posture was rigidly messianic as he stood with legs apart and arms spread-eagled towards the sun. His long body was pale and emaciated. He wore blue nylon swimming trunks and heavy white shower clogs. He began to sing a morning mantra, his voice low and melodious, his eyes squeezed shut.

"I'm not into hostility," she said.

"I'm not either," I said.

"I think you are. Just a little."

"How so?" I asked.

"Well, you want me off this board." Her voice suddenly rose to a higher pitch. "You lie on this board like you think you own it. No good. No good. I'm sick of that kind of attitude. I'm up to here with that kind of chicken shit. Just the way you slouch over it and hang one leg over the side and wrap yourself up in that sheet makes me sick. It makes me want to puke. I can't stand guys like you. You can see I need help and you just lie there thinking you're some kind of laid-back local star. . . ."

She stopped. I wanted to get rid of her but I didn't know how to go about it. If I had been able to choose someone to share this particular morning with it wouldn't have been her. It might have been someone with the kind of suspicious repression it takes to share a small space with. Someone a little older.

The door to cabin nine opened and two girls in red panties and black bras took long wavering steps towards the pool and then sat down. They were followed by a black man in white shorts and blue tank shirt. He stared at the top of their curly blond heads and then returned to the cabin. An elderly man with a towel wrapped around his thick waist stepped outside cabin ten and whispered to the two girls, who stared at the pool. His long white hair was tied behind his head with a pink ribbon and he slapped a TV antennae against his thigh. He waited for a long moment but the girls held their gaze. Then he walked over to the edge of the pool, to the left of the diving board, and yelled to someone at the far end.

"It's a fucking earthquake. It might get worse. I can't move them. They're scared out of their minds."

A wheezing voice called back. "Just get them out of the doorway. Forget about the date. It's only a grand. Get them cooled down. I don't care how you do it. Give them some reds if you have to."

The man looked into the water. Then he shifted his gaze to the end of the diving board and spoke vaguely towards us.

"Everyone is so snapped out because they

don't know how to handle disasters. Someone says dying to them and they put their heads under the bed. I never saw the likes of it. This is the worst goddamn shithole place I've ever seen. You don't see it at first because of all the palm trees and orange juice bars but let something happen and then see what they do. There could be a million dead and maimed out on the roads and no one would pay it any mind. I swear to god. Look at the two of you; balling and playing around out there like you was movie stars. All you need is a color TV and some goof balls and you'd be wailing. Now ain't that the truth? I'm getting my kids out of this place if I have to leash them and walk them out."

"Yeah, you're right," the girl said.

The man zapped the antennae against his thigh and walked past the two girls, who were staring at their feet. He slammed the door to his cabin.

He had reminded me that I was on a diving board. I had forgotten and that was no small achievement. Perhaps I needed another tremor to block it all off again. The girl had removed her tee shirt and was vaguely rubbing her right breast while staring off across the pool. The sheet had fallen from my shoulders and gathered itself around my waist and legs. I propped myself up on my elbows. The ends of the sheet had fallen into the pool so that now there was a slight weight tugging at my lower body. The sun was rising underneath the neon motel sign. Its presence made me almost relaxed. A few cars moved slowly on Santa Monica Boulevard and I took that as a good sign. And yet there were a few dead around. There was even one in my bathroom.

A tight lipped, parched young couple with straw cowboy hats and khaki shorts carried their bags out from cabin twenty-four. They dropped them to my right, at the edge of the pool. The bags were new and cheap. They sat on them and stared blankly into the pool. The woman wore a large shell necklace which she twisted slowly through her fingers while her husband tossed a silver key in the air. The key picked up the rays of the sun and occasionally fell through his fingers to land with a brittle clink on the cement. The pool area had become congested. People moved in and out of cabins, slamming doors and yelling at each other, while some sat quietly, as if adjusted to whatever might come. I began to suffer a strange nausea as if I was being pulled towards a forbidden place deep within myself, a swamp that I had only reached a few times before. We were becoming removed from the pool, from the calamity which we had been unable to confront.

"What's your name?" she asked.

"I don't know," I said. "I mean, I don't know how to answer that."

I was suddenly afraid of losing the anonymity that existed between us, as if once we knew our names the erotic focus we were falling into would dissolve. I curled my lower lip.

"We're overloaded as it is."

"Yeah, you're right," she said.

An upright middle-aged man in white slacks and yellow polo shirt walked out of cabin eight. He shook his head, disappointed in the surroundings. He circled the pool twice, carrying a black leather briefcase and whistling tunelessly. He stopped once and stared at us. His small pugnacious face twisted into a frown. He walked to the office and barked an order.

"Clear the area. The quake isn't over. All you people are in danger out there."

One of the two girls outside cabin ten went inside.

"This area is hazardous," he shouted.

The tight lipped woman with the straw cowboy hat looked up from her vigil by the pool.

"Fuck off, Jack," she said evenly.

The man turned on his heels and disappeared into the office. A helicopter circled overhead. There was a sudden tremor and then a deafening crash as power lines snapped on Santa Monica Boulevard and a car swerved into the plate glass window of a luncheonette. The window in the office broke and glass sprayed out towards the pool. The golden haired man in the blue swimming trunks, involved in a wavering shoulder stand, dropped to the ground and dove into the pool. The girl put her hand on my cock and I had an erection. She crawled out on the board and put her arms around me and we kissed.

Part of the edge of the pool must have caved in. I could hear a man weeping. A woman on the second story landing shouted for Harold. Feet ran around the pool, there were distant thuds behind me, a door opened and fell off its hinges, two women chanted the Lord's Prayer while a man yelled at them to shut up. A fire engine clanged down Santa Monica Boulevard followed by police and ambulance sirens. The diving board was still, as if we had been overlooked. Her tongue explored my mouth and her hands wandered over my thighs and stomach. The sheet had slipped to my ankles. I opened my eyes. Her eyes were still closed and a line of sweat had broken out on her forehead. She was trying to struggle out of her pants while keeping one hand on my cock.

Two men, naked except for brown leather shorts, ran out of cabin fourteen. The one with long blond hair carried a video tape machine. The other was completely bald and carried a tape recorder with one hand while dragging an hysterically laughing girl with the other. Her long red hair hid her face and she was naked except for an elastic bandage around her left leg. The remaining girl from cabin ten pulled her down beside her and gently stroked her hair. The two men strode to the edge of the diving board. The one with the video tape filmed the pool and the surrounding chaos. The other dropped his tape recorder and took a small notebook from his pants pocket. He began to write. I shut my eyes, trying not to experience anything outside the diving board, but their voices slipped through.

"I can't get the focus."

"Shoot anyway."

"We should have a movie camera."

"It's a drag. The sound is all fucked up."

"Do you see that one over there? Jesus Christ."

"I got to get some sound."

"Forget sound. It's all in the pictures."

"Can you get that old one? Yeah, follow him. Wow, that's all for him. Get those two. Do you see those two on the diving board? Get closer. I don't believe those two."

My attention had strayed too far. There were voices now, and agony, radios, bells, screams, splashes, snaps, whirring cameras, information, orders. I was adrift in it all, excited and terrified at the panic, a part of the panic, and it strengthened my first infantile reaction to her. I couldn't jump in the pool. A crowd had gathered and some of them felt safe enough to stare at us. It turned us on. We plunged on. She had removed her pants. The sheet was covering my ankles but otherwise I was available. Her cunt had maneuvered itself to within inches of my cock. Sitting on my thighs she rubbed the top gently between her palms. It was amazing the way it sprang up. A grinding crash behind us sent the crowd away. Whatever ambivalence we might have felt about suddenly being in show business disappeared. The four ends of the sheet were suddenly pulled from underneath. I could only hold on and wait. We clung to each other while splashes of water sprayed over us. The two wheezing voices underneath the diving board were impossible to shut out.

"I got these corners tied. There's no room for you."

"I can't swim."

"Then drag yourself around the edge."

"Where will I go? You don't own this space. There's enough room for me to hang on."

"You can stand in the shallow end."

"It's too crowded. One of those freaky kids threw up and one looks already drowned. Listen, I can make it here. I won't cause no trouble. I'm afraid to get out of the pool."

"I don't give a shit what you do but if you don't get yourself off these sheets I'm going to put your head under the water for you."

The feeble one managed to splash away. She eased her way over my now half limp cock. She still had her eyes closed and I closed mine, allowing my cock to rise into her. The words around us blurred and carried no definition. I had been close to removing myself from words for a long time. It was no big deal. At that point I was more concerned about the pressure of the pulled sheet on my ankle. But at least the pressure served to ground me. The information of the earthquake, even as it was being shouted back and forth across the pool, was dropping away from us. Perhaps everyone in the pool was still in the thick of it, puking, splashing, dying, embracing. We had no doubt been forgotten. I didn't care one way or the other. She was definitely over me. She wasn't moving, content to contain and be contained. Fingers scratched beside my head as they tried to grasp the end of the board. The board was moving but it only removed and excited us. more. Water was splashing over us so that our own moves were slippery and wet. There was a great deal of groaning and struggling going on underneath the board. But there were the same sounds on the board as well. We were away. She had started moving. I heard the distant click of shutters, the whirr of cameras, the mutter of instructions. She bent forward, as if away from the scrape of small machines behind her, and held on to my shoulders. She licked my forehead. There was so much to forget in order to go on. For a moment I forgot. I had time until the sense of time returned. We didn't exactly abandon ourselves. I always knew where I left off and she began. But it was a surrender of sorts. I no longer felt words. I no longer said words. I no longer heard words. I no longer knew words, as if that was an ominous prelude for what was to come. And for a moment, even the earthquake, the catalyst towards our minor transgression, fell away.

It ended in the pool. The sheet was jerked around my ankles and the pain made me sit up. The movement threw her back, away from me, and even as she was trying to hang on to my shoulders, she was falling. At the moment of separation, I came.

She joined me, her mouth opening in rage as she bent slowly backwards, her eyes maniacal and pleading. There was finally only a foot and then that, too, disappeared. As I peered after her, a hand reached up and pulled me by the neck into the pool.

The sheets had formed a sling and I fell into the middle. I became entangled among three or four other bodies as they thrashed among the sheets and tried to climb onto the diving board. I was struck several times on the face and shoulders and began to lose consciousness. I didn't resist. I had no special thoughts. Then I saw the back of the girl's head and I reached out to grab her hair. A hand shoved me under the water again. A foot stepped on my shoulder trying to reach the diving board. I was at the bottom of the sling and I had no air left. I slipped over the sling and fell to the bottom of the pool, which I discovered was only five feet deep because of all the water draining out. I stood up and looked around.

There were fewer people. The man in the straw cowboy hat still sat by the pool but his wife wasn't next to him. His key was gone and his hands were folded passively in front of him. Two firemen pulled a hose through the office. Above the office rose tiny flames and a thick cloud of smoke. Beyond that cloud there was a larger, thicker one. The girl swam slowly to the other side of the pool, her form delicate and poised as if she was pretending to be Esther Williams. The golden haired man swam after her and helped push her up onto the cement.

She lay on her stomach as he pulled himself up beside her. On the diving board two men in wet trousers sat back to back and slammed their fists down on the fingers that reached up from underneath. The figures in the sling seemed unaware of anything else around them, as if the battle for the diving board had erased their memories of the event that had thrown them there. I tried to draw myself out of the pool but my arms had lost their strength. Black cordovan shoes were parked in front of me. I pulled one of the laces.

"Stop that," a voice said.

I looked up. He was looking down. He seemed official because his blue gabardine suit wasn't wet or even disarranged. His thin mustached face was stern and authoritative. I held onto his shoe.

"Help me up," I said.

He looked down at me paternally. "You're safer in the pool. Jumping in like that might have saved your life. You should wait until the proper kind of help comes before you climb out. You're in shock."

"Help me up," I said.

He looked away, towards the other side of the pool.

"You creepy son of a bitch," I yelled. "Help me out of the goddamn pool."

He tried to step back but I held on to his foot. He tried to kick my hand away with his other foot but I held on.

"Let go or I'll kick your face in," he said quietly.

I reached up with my other hand and pulled him towards the pool. To one side I could see a man on his hands and knees, bent over with hysterical giggles.

"If I fall," the man said, "I'll drown your ass."

I pulled him in. It felt somehow obscene and a little corny to spend these moments pulling and pushing. He fell over me. When his head emerged he made no effort to move towards me. He stared blankly around him. Then he turned and waded towards the sling. On the other side of the pool the golden haired man slowly rubbed the girl's thighs and legs. She seemed lifeless. He rubbed her ass and she bent her legs a little as if whe wanted him to enter her. The man in the straw cowboy hat walked over to them. As the golden haired man was bending to kiss her upper thigh, the man with the straw cowboy hat threw himself on top of him. They rolled on the ground, kicking and biting. The girl jerked away and drew her legs up to her chest. She stared vacantly across the pool. I turned around and climbed out of the water.

I lay exhausted on the wet cement. There was a slight tremor, nothing substantial, but it was enough to set off a chorus of screams from the people around the pool. It was also enough to start me off in a lurch towards my cabin.

I walked in and shut the door. Plaster had fallen on the floor and a lamp was overturned but otherwise there was a neutral feeling to the room. The body still lay over the doorsill of the bathroom. I walked into the bedroom and put on the blue

25

jeans that were on the floor and a red tee shirt. I shoved my feet into a pair of sandals and went outside again.

I walked into cabin five. I was afraid to be around people but I couldn't stay in my room. An old white haired couple with newspapers and notebooks on their laps sat on the only two armchairs. Five young men sat cross-legged on the floor in jockey shorts. They seemed very serious. The youngest, who was about fourteen, cried silently. Two younger girls, who looked exactly alike with long blond hair and smooth round faces, lay curled in front of the couch in blue flannel nightgowns. In front of the television set lay an English sheepdog, his head crushed and bloody and one leg broken. The white haired couple sighed in unison and wrote slowly in their notebooks. No one noticed me except for the lady in the straw cowboy hat and shell necklace. She sat on the couch and drank bourbon from a bottle.

"I thought you drowned," she said. She took a drink and looked down at the floor.

The old man removed small silver rimmed glasses and rubbed his eyes. His thin patriarchal forehead was lined with wrinkles and deep furrows. With the thumb and forefinger of one hand he pulled a button off his tan African safari jacket.

"We can't get the news," he said gently. "We can't do anything until we know exactly what the situation is."

One of the young men, his face pale and

vulnerable, paced from the couch to the television set and back. He wore a sagging red bandana around his long black hair and covered his prearranged space with short precise steps, pausing to gather in a deep breath as he reached the couch or television set. As he completed his turn he gestured with his right hand, chopping down and out.

"That's the trouble with this family," he said violently. "We always bullshit around and discuss things and whatever happens passes us by. We're not going to have a situation like this again. We can wipe out half a billion dollars' worth of communications in six hours. It's chaos out there. They won't know who we are. The police and army will be looking for survivors. We'll never have an opportunity like this again. There's no such thing as news. We're being castrated while we wait around for the news. That's all a hype. Look at you, your whole life has been devoted to interpretation and analysis. It's been a total failure."

He sat down near the dead dog.

"You miss the point." The old man spoke without emotion, his voice weary and detached.

"Then just what the hell is the point?" the young man asked. He knocked his knuckles on the dog's stiff foreleg.

"The point is that you're so hopelessly deluded and romantic. You always have been. You think in nineteenth-century terms and that together with not being able to get it up represents a danger to us all."

"OK, do it your own tight assed way," the young man muttered. He lay down with his head on the dog's stomach. "But you're full of shit. I just want you to know that."

The old woman reached over and touched her husband's shoulder. She spoke in a quiet melodious voice.

"I do think the problem of information is, at least for us, dear, an anachronism. We mustn't forget that one of our collective problems as a family has been to divorce ourselves from the definitions we have inherited. Charley is not altogether wrong, although his style and rhetoric are certainly embarrassing."

She sat back and closed her eyes.

"Fuck you, Mother," Charley said passively.

"You already have, dear," his mother replied without opening her eyes.

The young man next to Charley began to speak and then stopped. He was younger than the rest. His hair was short, his lips thin and compressed.

"Go ahead, Adam," the brother next to him said. He put his fingers on Adam's upper thigh and rubbed gently. He kept his fingers working while he lay back and shut his eyes. He was heavy set, with a thick black mustache and sullen lips. Adam put his hand over his and they rubbed together.

"Well, I think we need more information." Adam paused as if to see if he had anyone's attention. "There might be millions dead out there. At first we were just going to rip off the media but I don't think blowing up things will do any good. I mean, we're liable to get offed ourselves. The other way it was only jail."

"Maybe we can still do it the other way," the mother said, opening her eyes.

"No way," Charley said. "There's not going to be any televison. The stations are caved in. It'll be a week before they get it together."

"What are you all going to do?" asked the lady with the straw cowboy hat. The family looked at her as one unit. She seemed to shrink under their steady gaze.

"I just came in here," she explained. "It was chance, you know what I mean? My husband is paralyzed out by the pool. He just sits there and smiles at everyone. He's already crapped in his pants. It was pure chance I came in here."

The father opened his arms in a wide expansive gesture.

"We have room for all," he said wearily. "We try not to set our own limits."

"Well, then," she persisted, "what are you aiming to do?"

"We're a singing family," Adam said shyly. "All except for Daddy who's a scholar on Turkish mosques. But he sings too, at least when he has to. He'd like to get out of the whole thing but Richard works him over good whenever he makes a move to leave."

Richard lay sleeping with his head propped up against the wall. He wore a green Tyrolean hat and a heavy gold bracelet on one wrist. His face looked smooth and innocent in repose. His body was totally hairless.

"Yeah," the lady with the straw cowboy hat said. "I know what you mean. But what are you planning to do?"

"We were signed up on this live program," Adam explained patiently. "It was a Sunday night special with other singing families. Only we were going to get on and fuck like crazy. We've been practicing and we figured we had a good chance to pull it off. It's our way of changing the structure."

"Your way, maybe," Charley muttered.

"We voted on it," Adam said. He lay back and let his brother slowly jerk him off. The woman with the straw cowboy hat sank against the wall and passed out. There was a loud tremor and plaster dribbled down from the ceiling.

"An aftershock," the father said. "It will be like this all day."

"Don't you think we should venture outside?" the mother asked. "We haven't been out once."

The other brother, who had been so silent and still that I hadn't noticed him even though his shoulder was touching mine, suddenly spoke:

"All our plans are vulgar and obscene. Blowing up power plants, filming destruction, fucking on TV—it's all an indulgence. We're in the middle of an earthquake and we're not dealing with who we are, what we feel. I say this is a piss poor family. The only thing that holds us together are projects. But they don't get us any money. What the hell use is it if we don't live decently. Look at this goddamn motel. It's full of trash. We don't know if we belong to the city or the country. We just keep on the move. When we're in the city we start to talk country and sing the blues and shit in the open. When we're in the country we talk big and read magazines and put everything down. Who gives a fuck what's happening on the next street or the next forty acres over. They're fighting in the streets, that's what they're doing. We're not making any move to grow, to figure out enlightened strategies. Why not go out and loot and then get the hell out? The fucking will take care of itself. It's overrated anyway. I say loot and plunder and think of the next twenty years."

He never moved. He opened his fat lips and the words came out in a low monotone. He was tall and dark and he wore a patch over one eye and carried his left arm in a black silk sling.

Richard crawled over to his mother and put his head on her lap. An explosion broke one of the window panes facing the pool. No one moved. A large man in blue coveralls with black soot on his face and plaster over his arms and shoulders ran into the room. He stood panting and looking wildly at the door.

"You can't stay in here," he yelled. "You people are in danger. Twenty-seven fell in and the office is totally smashed. You don't have to worry about the bill. I know you've been here two months but just get packed and get out. We can't worry about the insurance."

He stood as if frozen. Two emaciated young

men in white chino pants slipped into the room and sat down on the floor in front of me. One carried an electric guitar with the cord dragging behind it and the other held an old harmonica with both hands.

"Safe enough here," said the one with the guitar. His head snapped back and he fell against my leg. His red hair was wet and the color was running out of it.

"It don't matter none to me," said the one with the harmonica. He pursed his lips and blew into the harmonica but no sound came out. His face was potato shaped with the features squashed in towards the middle.

"There ain't nowhere to go anyway," he said.

"That's the way I see it," said the one with the guitar.

"I stopped believing those broadcasts," said the one with the harmonica. "You hear the guy with the bullhorn?"

"No."

"He didn't know what was happening. He was crouched down there underneath a truck with his head underneath a raincoat just getting off from his voice."

"Yeah." The one with the guitar lay back and propped his feet on the dead dog. "We should get to a hospital," he said morosely. "With all them lamed and crushed out there we could steal us five years' worth of dope."

"They done beat us to it. . . . Hey?"

"Yeah."

32

"Hey, I'm on the way out. The dizzies are coming on me and I can't see correct."

"You might as well fall out," said the one with the guitar. "No sense hanging out today."

They both closed their eyes.

A young woman in pressed gray slacks and jersey rushed into the room and counted the occupants. She put the number down on a yellow legal pad. She tried to light a cigarette but her hands were shaking and the match went out. She sank down by the door and bit her tongue.

The room was getting very crowded. Three or four more people jammed in. I recognized a woman's neck and red dress. People were standing and sitting in front of me and I could distinguish various objects and parts of bodies—a black and blue leg, a sniffling nose, a nodding head in front of my sandals, a broken arm, the old man's glasses on the floor and then a black boot grinding them into the rug. The golden haired man in the blue nylon swimming trunks wandered by, his face petulant and animated, smiling and nodding as if he was the host at a large cocktail party. He moved up to the man in the coveralls and whispered in his ear. The man backed away, his face averted, trying to make it to the door. The door opened again and a young intern holding a syringe looked anxiously in the room and then walked away. Perhaps someone had started a rumor that it was safe in cabin five or that the Red Cross was handing out doughnuts and coffee. Two small and finely featured drag queens in torn Chinese silk dresses squeezed through the door followed by a large woman in an open blue dressing gown with her hair half up in curlers. The woman with the straw cowboy hat woke up, her jaw slack and her eyes glazed. She sat directly across from me and I had time to see her reach up and bite a man's thigh before the view was blocked by two men arm wrestling. A woman wept and others joined in. A struggle broke out and a glass was broken and someone was pushed over the couch. I was in danger of being crushed as people pushed towards the door. But the door was stuck or it had been locked from the outside. The family joined hands and burst into "Ruby Lips Are Forever." They sang in lusty high pitched voices. The crowd quieted down so that there was only a general milling around and a few sniffling complaints from the wounded. The family followed right away with "Only You" and then a fast tempoed "Seafood Mama." I sang as loud as possible and shouted a few requests. People began to slowly relax and actually expand. They touched each other and made a few shy moves towards caressing and groping. The twin girls had woken and one was kissing the man in the blue coveralls while the other was unzipping his fly. They were singing and smiling. I stood up. A strange and delirious energy had seized the room. Limbs and torsos were engaged in various combinations accompanied by heavy groans and sighs. There were creakings and squeezings, blind snatches and smackings. Openings were spat into and massaged, cocks and cunts were rubbed and labored over. It was all done without words, with eyes closed, as if in slow motion or under water. I tried to single out individual moves but I wasn't able to make distinctions. My pants were reached into from the rear and a long finger wriggled up my ass. I couldn't handle a response. I shrugged off the searching finger with a frenzied dip of my ass and moved away. I was starting to hammer on the door when it opened from the outside and sunshine flooded past three firemen with hoses. I stepped outside as they stepped in.

The morning was hot. Clouds of smoke billowed over the Hollywood Hills. It was quiet around the pool. No one was in the water and the diving board was occupied by the man in the straw cowboy hat who sat with his arms around his legs, rocking back and forth. Mattresses had been dragged out of the cabins and lay scattered about in a foot of dirty water. People huddled on the mattresses like war refugees and two Red Cross ladies, with white uniforms and stiff blue hats, splashed among them offering Coke for a dime and coffee for a nickel. They were picking up a nice piece of change. The girl lay sprawled across a mattress on the other side of the pool. Her head rested on a black doctor's bag and her feet were propped up on a television set. Someone had thrown a blanket over her legs but the rest of her was naked. She looked half dead. On the mattress adjacent to hers three young boys worked out a song with two guitars and a bongo drum. The sirens had become a steady sound and I no longer listened to them. I walked down to Santa Monica Boulevard.

The sewers had been ripped open and the heavy smell of shit and rotten gas burdened the air. The street had buckled down the middle. Glass and masonry were scattered everywhere. Two water mains poured out rivers of water while electric cables sparked and snaked over the wreckage. I walked towards the luncheonette up the street. A red Chevrolet had gone half way through the plate glass window. There was a Kansas license plate on the back and a plastic Jesus on the dashboard. A man's head was half way through the windshield. Someone was inside, fixing sandwiches and hustling around. The smell of coffee overwhelmed me. I picked up a piece of lead pipe and threw it through the remaining glass. I didn't try to explain the act to myself. A round Mexican in a white apron and chef's hat stepped through the door.

"You no like the door, eh, cocksucker?" He smiled broadly. "You got the spirit of the times. You understand what to do. When she blow you got to blow."

He ducked back into the luncheonette. Two men in yellow hard hats were eating sandwiches at the counter. A group of musicians or junkies or college kids were sitting at a table, sipping coffee

and eating hard boiled eggs and pastry. There were
five of them and they wore gray sweat shirts and
long handlebar mustaches. They seemed com-
fortably stoned, and two, in fact, had nodded out. A
second table was filled with neighborhood cus-
tomers, families who had run screaming out of their
homes, clutching their silverware and teddy bears.
Some still wore pajamas and nightgowns while
others labored under raincoats, wool hunting
jackets, galoshes and ski pants. They ate with
abandon from plates heaped with potato salad,
jello, cole slaw and tuna fish salad. The Mexican
scurried everywhere, filling coffee cups and keeping
the plates full. When a plate was empty and more
food had been absolutely refused he smashed it
against the wall. He laughed and sang in Spanish
and drummed two spoons against the formica
counter. No one paid any attention to him.

"This is the very last meal," he sang out. "Sí,
sí. This is one monster of a disaster and the country
is over. Who is not to say that? . . .Olé!"

A short man in artificially faded jeans and
black cowboy boots and a pink and white Western
shirt shouldered his way past me. In front of him on
a silver leash pranced a white German shepherd
carrying half an arm in his mouth. I followed them
in and stood by the counter.

"How you doin, Lorenzo? You greasy spick."
He rapped his fist on top of a hard hat and took a
seat at the end of the counter.

"Yessir, boys, this is one helluva mess. A tree

37

fell through my Pontiac and my house is done smashed up like a bomb hit it. Knocked my De Kooning off the wall and broke up all that slant art I got collected. Reminds me of War Two only this one is more purely loco. More like a civil war. They're running berserk down the street, shooting at each other and carryin' on. Melrose has declared war against Wilshire. I like to go on down there myself. I got me an old Winchester 30 that could raise some dust. Hey Lorenzo, how's fer bacon and eggs up?"

"No hot stuff," Lorenzo yelled. He poured a cup of coffee and set it in front of him. "We got cold stuff today." He giggled and threw a glass at the front fender of the red Chevrolet.

"Gimme anything," the man said. His hands were shaking and he had to bend over and slurp the coffee up with his mouth. The dog curled up under his stool and chewed on the arm.

"You figure they'll send the soldiers out?" Lorenzo asked.

The man's head shot up: "I don't know why not. But this is some show, ain't it? We got the attention of the world fixed on us now, boy. The skyscrapers downtown toppled over and one hundred thousand got killed on the Santa Monica freeway. And it wasn't even rush hour. I seen one man drop dead on the street because his heart gave out on him. Couldn't stand all the excitement. Nothing hit him. Ah, shit, Lorenzo, he was my buddy, that's who he was. My new buddy."

He slumped to the counter. I took a plate from a table and helped myself to potato salad and pickles.

"No pay today," Lorenzo shouted. "Everything and everybody free today."

I went back through the broken window carrying my plate. The back door of the car had been wrenched open and I stepped inside and sat down. The seat was full of fishing equipment, comic books and a *Stars' Guide to Hollywood*. I ate my potato salad and leafed through *Superman*. I was hungry and felt like going back for more. Lorenzo beat me to it, shoving a plate of chicken salad through the door and taking my other plate and smashing it on the roof of the car. I shoveled it in with my fingers, without looking up. When I finished, I lit a cigarette and sat back. I figured it must be eight o'clock, nine at the outside. It was peaceful in the car, almost too peaceful, but something unaccountable and weird had been released inside me, a manic carnivorous force that was causing the muscles around my mouth to twitch uncontrollably. I had no memories. Yesterday didn't exist. Hallucinations slid towards and through me. I tried to leave the car but I couldn't move. My hands were shaking and I was nauseous. I threw the fishing line out the window with a hook and sinker on the end of it. I thought I might be able to snag myself a doughnut. The hook lodged

into a table leg and the angle of the window left me
no room to free it. The two yellow hard hats walked
by, carrying picks and shovels. A large florid face
looked in on me.

"Any luck?"

"No luck. Not so far."

"You should be using a different lure. Now if it
was me I'd throw in a hand grenade and just lie
back and watch the food land on my plate."

He tugged the line and grinned.

"I just might try that," I said. I tried to find
something else to say, to joke along, but no words
came out.

"Feel like diggin?" he asked.

I nodded.

"Come on then," he said. "We need all the
help we can get."

He offered me a hand and I grasped it. He
pulled me out and I leaned on the rear fender. They
looked me over.

"You're shaken bad," the other one said. "But
you might make it if you get into digging. When the
shakes get too bad just sink down and throw it all
up. But you're digging. You don't got no choice. We
just enlisted you."

They slapped me on the shoulder, gave me a
belt of bourbon and handed me a shovel. We
walked down Santa Monica Boulevard, three
abreast, our shovels over our shoulders, our arms
swinging loosely. We whistled "Onward, Christian

Soldiers." A few others joined us, crawling out from collapsed buildings and overturned cars. They fell in behind and we formed a loose formation. A few carried hunting rifles and one wielded a long kitchen knife but mostly we just dragged ourselves along. Soon we were a group of fifty and we were all whistling. We passed several buildings that had completely caved in but no one made a move to dig. Small groups of survivors stared without emotion as we marched past. The more desolation we saw the more contained and energetic we seemed to become. One of the hard hats stepped out to the side and hollered at us:

"All right you sloppy assed excuses for human beings, close up the ranks."

We did as we were told, stiffening our shoulders and lengthening our stride. We began to march like inspired recruits and when anyone fell out we stepped over him without a glance. He was gone forever. A voice behind me shouted:

"Count cadence, count!"

"Hup twop treep foh." We yelled out the army cadence. After we had shouted it out a few times, there was a soft sigh among the ranks. Our spirits dropped, like all conscripts', and yet we moved along, our eyes on the ground, somehow unable to abandon the order that had been laid on us. The hard hats stopped in front of us and we sat down around them. We were in front of a ten story apartment building. The side facing us was completely exposed. A rescue crew was already digging at the rubble. Most of the lower floors had fallen in. The building was expensive and tasteless in a clean pretentious way and even the roots underneath the slabs of lawn that had been torn and opened seemed arranged and synthetic. To one side of the ripped blue awning stood a rococo statue of a naked Venus. The head was missing and one arm was broken above the elbow. Masonry and plaster still dribbled to the ground. Workers had tunneled into the debris and a few inhabitants had been rescued. They sat huddled on a bright sliver of untouched lawn. Two helmeted but shirtless policemen spoke over walkie talkies and a helicopter circled overhead. I tried to touch the man next to me on the shoulder but he shrugged violently and moved away. A stove that had been leaning precariously over the edge of the seventh floor dropped straight down and buried itself a foot into the lawn. A heavy set black in bermuda shorts and sandals stretched out next to me. He was sweating and twisting a large ruby ring on his finger.

"Fuck all this digging," he said. "I don't like holes. They come and rousted me out of where I was safe in the laundromat playing cards and then marched me up to dig for some high roll asshole that's buried alive in his seventy grand set of walls. Not this child."

He stepped over me. He stood for a brief

moment looking at the building and then walked quickly away.

A hard hat appeared in front of me. "We have to get down to where they are."

He gestured for me to follow him.

"I don't have to get down to where they are," I said.

"I'm saying you do." He stepped closer. His face was black with soot and grime and a bloody gash streaked across his forehead and half way down one cheek. He stared at me until I looked away. I followed him past the awning to the entrance of the building. The mailboxes and front desk had been smashed in. An old woman in a pink slip sat among hundreds of envelopes, tearing them open and looking for money. The rest of the entrance was completely buried. A dozen men worked with shovels and pick axes but their efforts appeared futile. I shoveled for a while, just to appear busy, but I was ready to split or fake being a casualty. I told myself it didn't matter if I kept busy although I knew that it did matter and that I was too tied up to do anything else. I knew that anything I thought about myself was bound to be bullshit so I kept on shoveling. There were a few bodies piled near us. We worked quietly until a cop ran into the entrance and shouted:

"Five men. We'll try the other side of the building."

A few of us followed him. The other side of the

building was leaning over at an angle but was otherwise untouched. The cop tried the door but it was jammed. I broke a window with my shovel and crawled inside. No one followed. They had opened another door. I was in a dining room. I opened the yellow drapes and sunlight poured through the windows. The floor was made out of shiny parqueted wooden squares. There was a round white marble table with black wrought iron chairs set around it. I went into the next room. The kitchen was full of broken glass and china and two pieces of white bread were still in the toaster. There was shooting outside. I ran into the dining room and looked out the window. A man sat slumped against the wall beneath me. He was looking curiously at a hole in his shoulder. He wore a blue and gold doorman's uniform and the features in his narrow pasty face were squeezed together in agony.

"I been shot," he said.

"Who did it?" I asked.

"How the fuck do I know who did it?" he said. "I been shot, that's all. There are guys running around shooting at people. Lunatics."

I crawled out the window and bent down beside him. He was bleeding all over the place. I took off my tee shirt and tried to fashion a rough bandage around him. Men crawled out through windows and from behind piles of debris. They walked cautiously over.

"I've been shot," the man said to himself.

"Honey, I been shot through the shoulder."

"Now they're shooting us," said a fat man in blue shorts and a red baseball cap. "There are maniacs out there fighting a war. Whole gangs running around killing themselves, looting and shooting off their guns. The cops are just crazy. You can't trust em. They're just out for themselves. I saw them gun butt a guy and then pistol whip him."

"Hand grenade!" someone shouted.

An explosion a few hundred feet away sent bricks and mortar flying down on us.

I dove through the broken window. Three others fell in after me. There were more shouts and then the chopping whir of a descending helicopter. We lay on our stomachs underneath the round marble table.

"It's every man for himself now," said the man with the red baseball cap. "I ain't shittin ya, this is it. I never thought I'd see the day. I come here from Ohio and I never expected this."

"It'll calm down," said a man in a white hospital attendant's uniform. "We've just never had a tragedy like this before. Folks aren't used to it."

He went over to the water cooler by the kitchen door and cupped himself a handful of water. He seemed very cool and sure of himself until his hands began to shake and the water spilled before he could get it up to his mouth.

The third man sat against the wall, pointing a

pistol loosely in our direction and looking us over with a sly suspicious grin. He wore white tennis shorts and a torn navy blue sweater. He looked like a college athlete, with a muscular build and thick features set under short cropped blond hair.

"How do I know you guys are on the level?" he said evenly.

"Who's on the level?" screamed the hospital attendant. "We've all been through a disaster. Death, you know what I mean? But at least we aren't running around popping off people. How do we know you didn't shoot the guy outside?"

"I did shoot him."

He looked us over as if choosing which one he was going to eliminate first.

"Now then," he said in the same even voice. "Who are you with?"

"What's that?" yelled the man in the red baseball cap. He crawled over me so that I was between him and the man with the gun. "We've been through an earthquake and I can't find my wife and you're asking me who I'm with? What's that? What's that?"

His voice trailed off and he closed his eyes.

"What outfit are you guys with?" the blond man asked again.

"We're not on any team," I tried to say softly. "We don't belong to any outfit or club or any one section of the city. We never even saw each other before."

My voice broke and I yelled at him:

"We're in here because of the earthquake!"

He stared at me, his gun unwavering. "Well, all I know is that you're too far north. And anybody too far north I don't like."

"I'm not from any north or south," I said. "I don't know about these other guys."

"I'm dying," said the man outside the window.

He groaned and struggled up against the window. His hand reached inside the sill and the broken glass cut into his wrist.

"You'd better help me," he whispered. "It's on you if you don't help me. I'll make a mess."

"I don't want him attracting attention," said the blond man. He gestured towards me and the hospital attendant. "Get him in. But I'll be watching you. I'll blow your brains out if you split."

We lowered ourselves out the window and hauled him through. We laid him on the round marble table. He looked at us with soft bewildered eyes and then he died. We sat down on the floor again.

A square face underneath an army fatigue hat looked through the window.

"How many you got there, Hank?" he asked.

"Three. I shot one. I don't know who the hell these others are."

"We're moving into the hills. We can't hold this area. They're infiltrating all around us."

"What shall I do with them?"

"Suit yourself, only make it quick."

His head disappeared. The blond man shot the hospital attendant through the forehead. There was a burst of machine gun fire outside. He dove through the window without looking at us.

"Do you know what to do?" asked the man in the red baseball cap.

I shook my head.

"Is this a war or what?" He began to cry. "I thought this was an earthquake."

"I don't know what it is," I said.

We sat waiting for the other to make a move. I finally stood up and walked over to the water cooler. I knelt down and let the water splash over my head.

"Don't you dare leave me," he shouted. "I don't know what's going on."

"It's all right," I said. "I don't know what's happening either."

"It's not all right," he said. He dried his tears with the back of his hand and tried to pull himself together. "I don't even have a knife or club. Where are we gonna go?"

I stepped up to the table and hugged him. He clung to me, his breath heavy and wet on my neck. Then he pushed me away, striking out with both fists.

"Jesus Christ," he said angrily. "Take it easy. You're more afraid than I am."

I tried to reach out to him again but he backed towards the window. I wanted to touch the son of a bitch, to get him to hold me. Or to pummel him, to slap him around. I had lost control.

"Unnnnnnnhhh," I said, reaching for him. I wasn't able to form words.

"Holy shit," he said. "You've gone crazy. Listen, you stay here and I'll leave. I'll go for help or something. We'll have a better chance."

I suddenly felt better. I managed to smile at him. "Yeah, you'd better leave."

He poked his head out the window. "It was probably some kind of a mistake with that guy. Earthquakes do strange things to people. I read about them in some magazine. It was probably some National Guard people who got the wrong information and went a little berserk."

He raised one foot over the windowsill. "Hell, ten years from now it will all make sense. Five years from now. Five months from now the way things go these days."

He raised his other leg and sat for a moment on the windowsill. "People don't go around doing crazy things like shooting people without there being an explanation. You know what I mean?"

With an airy salute he dropped over the edge.

I hummed for a while, concentrating on one pitch and trying to keep it going. Then I shifted to a higher pitch. I walked around the table, humming. I went through the pockets of the dead man. I found cigarettes, a silver lighter and a leather billfold. The billfold held twenty dollars, an

American Express card and a faded picture of a small Chinese woman in a white dress about to send a bowling ball down an alley. I put it all in my pocket. Then I walked into the kitchen and opened the icebox.

The food was still fresh. I ate a mouthful of cold hamburger and drank lemonade from a plastic pitcher. I wiped a splash of lemonade over my forehead and went into the next room. It was a blue and pink bedroom with stuffed animals lying on the yellow satin pillows of the canopied double bed. I climbed into the bed and pulled the covers over me. I thought I could hear the whole building swaying and shifting above me. I grabbed a stuffed elephant and held it next to me. There was warmth enough but no safety. I heard distant shouts and then they were lost in an avalanche of disintegrating walls. The bed slid forward. A crack in the ceiling slowly widened and I was covered with white dust. Across the room a dresser slid through the door. Everything stopped and I lay very still. The ceiling had caved in over the windows and it was very dark. The air was stuffy and dense with tiny floating particles. I had trouble breathing. I felt my way forward, crawling over an iron pipe and sliding down a few feet of rough wood into a long tunnel that might have been the hall. I felt compelled to find some light, even if it meant climbing to a higher floor. I crawled up a flight of stairs or perhaps two flights, it was impossible to tell. I found myself in another hall where I could distinguish several shapes. I bumped against a washing machine or a dishwasher. I crawled around the shape but I was blocked by a smashed piano. The keys were lying on the floor and the legs had broken off. I crawled the other way, towards a dim light the size of a football. I eased up to the hole and looked down. Four bodies lay in a pool of oil three or four stories below. Paper backed books and a pile of women's dresses and blouses lay scattered over them. The floor creaked and I began to slide through, towards the widening hole. I crept backwards. There was a moan on the other side of the wall. There were whispers and then two short taps. I tapped back. There were two more short taps. I tapped four shorts and a long. Three short taps came back. I tapped five shorts and two longs. There was no answer. I tapped two longs and a short and there was a chuckle and three longs. I waited for a minute and then shot him two shorts and a long and he came right back with the same. I tapped once and he tapped once. I tapped four longs and a short and there was no reply. I might have offended him. I tried different combinations but there was still silence. Finally I called out: "Hello, hello." There was still no answer. I tapped again and I thought I could hear whispering. I called out "Hello, hello," again. There was silence. "Well fuck you," I said and crawled away. But then there were three shorts, a long and two more shorts.

I slammed my fist against the wall and yelled: "Waaaaaah." A clear gentle voice replied:

"I can hear you."

"Are you all right?" I asked.

"We're all right."

"How many are you?"

"Four," he said. "Four or five."

"Do you need help?"

"No. It's too late for help."

"Some of you must be all right."

"No. We've all had it. The others can't talk."

"I can talk," said a low woman. "We're doing fine. Just fine."

"I'm crawling around," I said. But I made no effort to move.

"We'll go through this one alone," the first voice said.

There was a long silence. Finally the first voice spoke:

"Are you there?"

"I'm here," I said.

"There should be stairs a little ahead of you. Maybe you can get to them. Was it an earthquake?"

"7.6 on the Richter scale."

He tapped again.

"Why are you tapping?" I asked.

"It's not me," he said. "Claire taps because there's a nerve jumping around in her broken arm. She's got a lot of anxiety."

"I'm coming around," I said.

"We don't want you."

"I have to try," I said. I started to crawl forward.

"Don't come," the woman's voice pleaded. "We know how to die by ourselves."

I crawled along the wall looking for an opening. There was tapping in back of me and then further ahead. I kept crawling forward but I couldn't find a break in the wall. The passage opened to the left and I followed it. The tapping faded. I tried to tap once more. There was no answer. Outside the building I thought I could hear shouts and the low grinding of a large machine being put into gear. I had no way of measuring the distance between myself and the open air. It might be a few inches. But the sounds were comforting, at least for a moment. I was seized by a sudden choking rage that just as suddenly changed into a whimpering melancholy. I needed sounds but because there were none I decided it was better to do without them, to cushion myself in my own enclosure, like a wounded animal. Except that I was suffocating and yelling for help. The building shook. I slid forward on my knees and elbows. It was darker and the passage had become even more pinched and narrow. I reached a wall. There was enough room to sit up. I banged on either side of me trying to establish boundaries. My fist broke through a thin layer of plasterboard. I reached through the wall and my fingers discovered two small bottles and a long piece of silk. I pulled the silk back through the hole and tied it around my waist. It felt like a woman's negligee. I pulled the bottles through. I opened one and swallowed a few pills. I tapped and yelled and tried to smash through the hole but I only managed to enlarge it by a few inches. I lay back and put my arms over my head and kicked at the ceiling. The ceiling was only three feet above me and I didn't have any trouble reaching it. Plaster showered down. I kicked again and there was an answering thump. I yelled and kicked and the thumps grew louder. I lay back, exhausted, my toes and ankles bruised. The thumps stopped as well. I was about to kick again when his voice stopped me:

"Why don't we try to talk it over?"

"I almost broke my toes trying to get through to you. Didn't you hear me yell?"

"You were kicking so I kicked."

"You might have laid up there forever if I hadn't yelled. You dumb asshole."

"Very true," he said quietly. "But we won't make it anyway. I make it ten to one odds. The next shock will take it all down."

"What'll we do?"

"Nothing."

"I've got one wall to kick yet."

"I'm better off than you. I got a big space up here. I might be able to get through to another room but I'm afraid to try."

"I don't believe you," I said. "You don't sound like you have a big space."

"You might be right," he said.

"I don't want to talk about it anymore," I said.

We were silent. He moved around and I could tell he had a bigger space. I kicked the wall behind me but it didn't give.

"Settle down," he said.

"We probably won't get out," I said. "But at least I have some pills."

"You have pills?" He sounded suddenly interested. "What kind?"

"Opium," I said. "A little bella donna. Some morphine."

"I could use some of that," he said.

"I'm saving it for when I make it out to the country. I'll wait it out there."

"Where?" I could tell he wanted to keep me talking.

"Up north. In Sonoma." I ad libbed a retirement plan. "I've got a little log cabin with a brook running by. No one around. When I make a move it's my move, you know what I mean? I got all the facilities."

I laid it on. I told him about the trout and the different trees and how cooled out the neighbors were. I described everything: the deer and vegetable garden, the pine floors and the sauna bath and the little guest cabin in back. I even told him how great it was to have a woman out there. He didn't say anything for a long time.

"Where are you from?" he finally asked.

"Hawaii."

"What do you do for money?"

"I can play a few instruments."

"I just want to make a connection," he said. "Maybe we can work something out. I'm from right here. Can you believe that? I live in this apartment. I have a wife and kid. They took off a few days ago to visit a friend in Santa Monica."

His voice trailed off. I heard distant shots. I either had to climb up to him or wait for another aftershock and hope I fell through to a safer place. He thumped above me.

"I'm pounding my way through," he yelled.

"I've got pills down here if you make it," I said. The floor gave a little. He was slamming on it with some kind of heavy tool. I shouted encouragement and slammed against the walls with my fists. A shoe pushed through the ceiling. I pulled on it with both hands. He screamed:

"I'm stuck."

He was stuck above the ankle. I undid his shoelaces and took off his shoe and sock.

"I'm screwed now," he said. "I can't move at all."

He wriggled around and pounded his hands on the ceiling, or, in his case, the floor. I pulled on his foot but it only secured and locked him in more. He screamed and twisted and finally he stopped. His foot was unusually long and thin and his toe nails had been clipped. I rubbed it down with the palms of my hands and it calmed him a little. The firing outside had increased. A hand rubbed the back of my head and I screamed.

"I live here." It was a woman's voice.

I turned around and pulled her to me. She pushed me away.

"Take it easy," she said. "We can get out. We just have to crawl back twenty feet or so and we can drop down to the next floor. That whole wall has fallen down. Maybe they have a net we can drop into."

"Who's that?" The man above us was screaming and wiggling his foot.

"It's me, Warren."

"Helena?" His voice was suddenly sober. "Are you all right? How did you get here?"

"I live here."

"I know that, you cunt." He started to get hysterical again. "I thought you were in Palm Springs. Mary told me you were in Palm Springs. How come you aren't in Palm Springs?"

"I had a fight with Saul and I left him."

"I always thought Saul was a loser."

"It doesn't exactly make any difference now, does it, Warren?" she said.

"Listen, Helena." His voice was rising again. "I know we never got along and I did you in that time in Manhattan Beach but you got to get me out of here. And stay away from that freak down there."

"Yeah, sure, Warren." She lit a match and peered into my face.

"He doesn't look like a freak to me," she said slowly.

"Don't joke around," he yelled. "Don't go crazy on me, Helena. I think my circulation is cut off."

"It always was, Warren."

We pulled away at the hole in the ceiling, digging at the plaster with our fingers. We managed to open the hole enough for him to pull his foot back.

"I'm going out with you," he said.

"We can't make the hole any bigger," I said.

Warren knelt over the hole and yelled: "You've been messing with my head ever since you got here. You don't even live in this goddamn building."

"Warren," she said patiently. "Listen to me. There are big beams on either side of the hole. You'll have to make it on your own."

"I'll die up here," he screamed. "I swear to god. If you pull out on me I'm finished. How do you like that, Helena? Finished."

I handed up the bottles. He grabbed my hand and held on. I pulled his hand through the hole and bit him on the wrist. He let go.

"Come on," she said. "We don't have any time. Let's not torture the poor fucker."

"Aspirin," he screamed. "Aspirin and vitamin C."

"We'll send someone," she said. "But try not to go out of your mind. Try jerking off or something."

"Bullshit. Bullshit. Bullshit," he yelled. His voice was going hoarse. "You're going to leave. You'll be sorry. Listen, come back here. I've got things up here you don't have. . . . Creeps. Murderers. Assassins. I hope you fall all the way through and break your lousy bones and they never find you but step all over you and smash your heads in with their shovels. They're fighting out there, did you know that? . . . Did you know that?"

His voice receded as I crawled after her. It took us over half an hour to crawl a hundred feet. We finally came to a large jagged hole. A dim light spread out a little from the hole and I could see her. Her dark hair fell to her shoulders and her narrow face was smooth and unlined. All the wrinkles had collected around her neck which had sagged into little wattles.

"You don't have to make an examination," she said. "I'm not a hooker. I'm an actress. You've seen me in a hundred pictures."

We concentrated on the hole. There was a ten foot drop but there was a couch beneath us. Two dead bodies lay on the couch and one on the floor. The bodies on the couch were naked and frozen in an awkward embrace. His arms circled her waist and his head was buried in her pubic area. His protruding ass was fat and pale compared to the rest of his body, which was darkly suntanned and muscular. Her head was thrown back over the couch and her eyes were still open, staring blankly up at us. Even though her hair was mostly white her body was firm and slender. One of her feet rested on the head of the man curled up on the floor. He was dressed in black silk pajamas and his face was pressed into the rug. Both of his hands clutched the ankle of the dead woman.

"I'd know that fat ass anywhere," Helena said. "But I don't know the rest of them. Bit players."

She closed her eyes. Her lips trembled and she held onto my arm with both hands. "I was always underneath him, never above him like this."

"We have to jump," I said.

"You first," she said.

I let myself fall onto the pile beneath me. I landed on the fat man's back and rolled to the floor. The floor threatened to give way but at the last minute it held. The ceiling had crumbled in back of the couch and along one wall, blocking the windows except for tiny probes of light which streaked across the room. A glass coffee table had smashed and the floor was covered with glass. I looked up at Helen.

"I can't do it," she whispered.

"Jump," I urged.

"No way." She shook her head.

She looked older from below. Her skeleton seemed to be pushing through her flesh.

"I'm not going to make it," she said. "I'm dead already."

"So stay up there," I said. "It's true. You don't have anything left. Your face looks like the bottom of a bird cage. Maybe you're what this is all about, to bring it all down and clean up all the disasters."

She stared at me, her mouth contracting, her eyes watering. I paced on the sinking floor.

Then she jumped, landing on the fat man's back. She held on and shut her eyes.

I crawled to the other side of the room and opened a door. I found myself peering down the side of the building. An army truck was parked below and men with rifles crept carefully through the piles of rubble. Everything was strangely silent. It was a beautiful clear day except for the huge clouds of smoke billowing up in the west. Bodies lay everywhere and the earth on the other side of the army truck had ruptured into deep chasms. The floor suddenly tilted to a forty-five-degree angle, sending the couch sliding towards the other wall.

"We can get out," I said. "It's only a two story drop. But there's something weird happening. There's an army truck out there and people crawling around with rifles."

I slid back to the couch.

"Don't push me," Helena said in a small child's voice.

"We have to jump once more," I said. "Then we'll be all right."

"Who are you, anyway?" she asked. "The earthquake didn't kill them. There's not a mark on them. How do you explain that?"

"I don't know." I was whispering as if there was someone else in the room.

"We're in some kind of war, aren't we?" She stroked my cheek. "I'm not exactly sure who you are. John Hodiak or Michael Rennie. Maybe Van Johnson. Some forties bimbo. An All-American second rater who does the right thing at the right time. You probably can get it up at the snap of a finger."

"That's me, all right," I said.

The floor underneath ours caved in. We clung to each other as the building swayed and bricks and plaster fell over us. Smoke drifted up through the floor and I could smell leaking gas. I tried to climb back to the edge but she pulled me back.

"I'm too wasted," she said. "Let's wait for a while. It won't fall anymore."

I pulled her hands off my legs.

"It's too far." She giggled hysterically.

I climbed towards the door. I held on to a pipe that stuck out of the floor and dropped my legs towards her.

"Grab my foot," I said. "Climb up beside me."

She grabbed my legs and held on. I grasped the pipe with both hands but she was a dead weight.

"I can't hold," I said.

'I can't either," she said. She slid back to the

couch. As I started to pull myself up to the edge and get ready to jump, she grabbed my ankles and I let go, falling back on top of her.

"It's hopeless," she said.

I hit her in the stomach. When her head came up I slapped both of her cheeks.

"You don't have the balls to leave me," she whispered.

The building started to collapse beneath us. I cupped my hands and she put her foot in them and stretched up to the pipe. She held on while I jimmied myself up. She used the pipe as a foot rest while I positioned myself beside her. We crawled up to the doorsill and sat with our legs over the edge.

"It's gone," she gasped. Her face seemed to regain its focus and her hands stopped shaking. "God, it's so awful," she said softly. "Everything's gone. There must be millions dead. I can't recognize anything. Oh god, where's Carol's building?"

We held hands and jumped onto the canvas back of the army truck. I fell all the way through and landed on the floor. Helena's back struck one of the metal ribs that held the canvas top together. She screamed and slowly slipped down head first into the truck. She landed on a stack of rifles. The men backed away from us, one of them pointing a forty-five at me. For a long moment there was silence. Then a heavyset man in tan slacks, pink cowboy shirt and white stetson walked up from the back of the truck and looked down at Helena. He wore a colt revolver in a snakeskin holster and slowly worked a wad of tobacco from one side of his mouth to the other.

"I'll be whipped," he said. "Where did you come from, darlin? Look here, Sam, appears like she dropped from the sky."

He nudged her with his boot but she was unconscious. Her leg was twisted and blood oozed out from behind one ear. I had a sprained ankle but otherwise I was unhurt.

"We jumped out of the building," I said.

The heavyset man turned to me. "And just what were you doing up there in that building?"

"I was part of a rescue team," I said. "I got trapped when the building started to give in. I found her up there."

"Well, now," he said softly. "Imagine that. Jumping from a building." His mouth formed a distant preoccupied smile. Then he suddenly kicked me hard on the right leg. "There aren't any rescuers in this area. We cleaned em all out. What do you think of that?"

"I think that's a good thing," I said.

"We're in control here and you might begin to wish otherwise." He took out a blue handkerchief from his hip pocket and wiped his perspiring brow. "We got ourselves dug in and established on Wilshire to the south and Sunset up on the north. We got La Brea on the east and we're working on the west. You look like you'd be one from the west. Listen here, boy, thousands of good people have been killed in the last hour on account of people like you. I don't want to hear no more about it."

His eyes focused briefly on mine and then shifted towards a small man in wire rimmed glasses. He was dressed in blood stained white yachting pants and a pale blue alpaca sweater. He carried a double barreled shotgun in both hands.

"Orville," the heavyset man said. "March em over to six and on the way back see if you can locate the fourth squad. They should have been back twenty minutes ago."

Orville gestured at me with the shotgun and I climbed out of the truck. We waited while two men carried out Helena.

"You'll have to put up with this until things get sorted out," Orville said. "We've had some unpleasant experiences with people in this neighborhood. People get confused and hysterical when faced with such a calamity. It's hard for them to know who to trust, who's looking after them and who isn't. They need a firm hand to guide them until everything calms down. We all have to start from the beginning now and discover who we are and what we're made of."

We walked down the road, the two men dragging Helena by her arms. It was impossible to walk in a straight line and several times we had to crawl over huge slabs of concrete and twisted pilings. After three hundred yards we left the road and walked towards a Texaco station whose roof had fallen in. I could no longer see the building we had been in or the truck. A man with a rifle in the crook of his arm leaned against an overturned station wagon in front of the Texaco station. He waved to Orville as we walked over to him. In front of him stretched a smooth expanse of lawn that had been cordoned off by a yellow nylon rope tied to stakes ten feet apart. The rope formed a rough circle about forty feet in diameter. In back of the circle were the remains of expensive colonial and modern homes. Three men lay on the lawn. Two of them lay face down with their hands tied behind them. The other lay propped up on his elbows, staring at us. I was told to sit inside the circle and not step out. Helena was dragged in after me and deposited at my feet.

"We'll keep you here for a while," said Orville. "It's for your own good. Most of the men haven't shown too much patience, even with suspects. When this whole mopping business is over we'll get you people categorized. I would advise you to stay where you are and not roam too near the edge of the circle. We've posted a few guards to discourage you. Later on we'll try and get in some hot food and have a doctor look you over. In the meantime settle down and try not to get too anxious."

He pivoted on his heels and walked away, followed by the two men who had carried Helena.

The man who lay propped up on his elbows looked at me. He was thin, his puffed and swollen face distinguished by a long handlebar mustache. A rough bandage had been tied around his shoulder and his white chino pants were muddied and blood stained.

"Do you know what this is about?" I asked.

"Do I know what this is about?" he asked himself slowly. "Well, hmmmmmm. They're rounding up people at random, shooting some and fucking around with the others. I was shot coming out of a record store on Sunset. Me and those two others tied up over there. We play country music together down at the Pig n' Whistle. We was ripping off some 8 tracks and these guys run in and yell at us to put up our hands or they'd shoot us. We didn't know who they were. I mean, why should we? Johnny and Kris ran off and they caught them and pistol whipped them something awful. I believe they were cornholed as well. Country style. There are three or four of these crazy groups trying to take over and run things. The cops are one. The spades are in there and some kind of cycle outfit. For all I know these people are Knights of Columbus or a bowling league."

The guard leaned casually against the overturned station wagon and bit the end off a cigar, then lit it. His eyes never left us. Another guard sat behind us on the other side of the circle, his back to a fallen elm tree, a rifle across his lap. In back of him smoldered the ruin of a white colonial house. Three men ran by the Texaco station, stopping and crouching into awkward positions, their rifles held in front of them. Then they ran on again. The guard by the station wagon turned and covered their direction with his rifle. One of them fell forward, exhausted. A shot rang out and ricocheted off one of the pillars of the colonial house. I lay face down, covering my head with my arms. A man lay in front of the circle, clutching at the short blades of grass.

"Appears like he should be inside with us," said the man with the handlebar mustache. He was still propped up on his elbows but then he slid forward and crawled across to the man lying outside the circle. The guard was crouching behind the overturned station wagon, staring off to the right where the shot had come from. The other men had disappeared. He slid underneath the nylon rope and reached out for the man's hand. The guard turned and motioned at him with his rifle, pointing back towards the inside of the circle. He crawled back inside the rope while the man on the ground sat up and dried his eyes with the back of his hand. The guard shrugged and looked away. The man picked up his rifle and stood up. He was talking furiously to himself. He was small and fat and his belly shook, as if his insides were out of control. He pulled his fatigue hat down over his forehead and spat on the ground. He walked over to the rope and yelled at us, looking over his shoulder to see if the guard was watching.

"You try anything like that once more and I'll blow you apart limb by limb. I've had enough of you people. I'm up to here. If it was up to me I'd line you all up now and shoot the lot of you. I'm talking to you, mister."

Neither of us answered. He walked away, mumbling something about faggots and winos. As he passed the guard he waved to him casually. When there was no response he broke into a wobbling sprint. The guard shrugged and watched him disappear behind the Texaco station.

"I'll tell you another thing," said the man with the handlebar mustache. He had resumed his position next to me. "They sent three astronauts up to the moon five days ago and they're due home today. God knows what kind of a reception they're going to get when they splash down. This might not even be an earthquake. Some foreign power might have blown up the whole works. The entire country might be totaled."

I crawled over to the men who were tied up.

"I wouldn't if I was you," he called after me.

I turned one of them over anyway. His eyes had been burned out and there was a flabby hole where his mouth had been. He was very young. I counted pieces of broken glass in front of me. I stopped at twelve and picked up a sharp piece of glass and drew blood from a finger. There was another tremor. The man with the handlebar mustache ran over to the rope. One leg was over it when the guard fired. The bullet struck near his foot and he fell backwards, into the circle. The tremor subsided and the guard stood up and walked over to the circle. He stood looking off towards the smoldering colonial house. His face was round and smooth. He wore silver granny glasses and the beginnings of a thin mustache over his upper lip. He stamped his foot and screamed down at the figure lying in front of him:

"Asshole! You don't want to leave here. You know what's happening to the people who are trying to leave this city? They're dying by the thousands, that's what. It's panic out there. Fucking chaos!"

"You tell em, Henry," the other guard called out behind us. "I'm with you, boy. Cripple the sons of bitches. They ain't no civilians. They saboteurs. That's what they are. Guerrillas."

Henry walked back to the overturned station wagon. The man with the handlebar mustache crawled back once more to where I was sitting. His wound had opened in his shoulder and blood was seeping through the bandage. His hands swept over the lawn gathering up glass and small pebbles into a pile. He knocked the pile down and then built it up again. Three men walked up Henry. They wore new fatigue hats and holstered forty-fives. Henry pointed to the west where the smoke had become thicker. One of the men pulled a hip flask from his jeans. He took a swig and passed it on. They spoke in low murmurs. The guard behind us walked slowly around the circle, his fingers sliding along the rope. He joined the others and took a long pull from the flask.

"What time is it?" I asked.

He continued to pile pieces of glass on top of each other and then knock them over. Then he spoke in a choking whisper:

"Time? You mean time, right? On the watch? Your girl friend all smashed up and we're on our way to a concentration camp and thousands dying everywhere and you want the time. The sun is overhead. That's time. No way to go now. Trigger finger punched in. Carburetor out. No wheels on the inside. You check the mask. You cheap bastard. Take it."

He took off his watch and threw it at me. It was 10:30. A helicopter skimmed across the ground from the east and the guards dove behind the overturned station wagon. The helicopter circled above them and a man leaned over and fired down with a burst from an automatic rifle. They fired back. Bullets shattered the cockpit and the helicopter swerved off in an oblique stuttering dive. It crashed a few hundred yards in back of the Texaco station and exploded. Two guards stood up. They finished off the rest of the flask and then dragged their three companions onto the grass, a few feet outside the circle. One guard squatted down near the bodies while the other ran off towards the south. It was hot. I crawled towards the western part of the circle, at a right angle from the guard. Then I turned and made my way along the edge of the rope towards him. When I reached him I threw him the watch and everything in my pockets and then put my hand over the line. He slipped the watch over his wrist and gestured at me with the rifle. He was about eighteen and his eyes were glazed and his mouth slack.

"No difference," he said.

"I'll probably be able to stand up and walk right over you in a few minutes," I said.

"No difference," he repeated. He held his rifle on me and his hands were steady. I crawled around the inside of the circle. There were dull explosions in the distance and the sudden whine of a chainsaw in back of the colonial house. I stopped half way around, up on the northwest section. I sat cross-legged and swayed back and forth while a large red wagon with automobile tires was slowly pulled towards the circle by four shirtless men. Bodies were piled on the wagon and when one fell off the men stopped to put it back on. Another fell off and they left it where it fell. They took a long time going around a deep crevice and coming back across the parking space in front of the Texaco station. They stopped a few feet in front of the circle. They were young and muscular as if they all belonged to the same college fraternity or water polo team. They lifted the bodies off the wagon and dropped them over the rope. There were sixteen bodies and they were all shot through the back of the head. I walked to the center of the circle. The man with the handlebar mustache was cutting his wrists with a large piece of glass. He was cutting very slowly and the blood oozed along his wrist and dripped slowly onto the pile of glass and pebbles in front of him. I sat down facing him, my back to the dead men.

"They really fucked it up this time," he whispered. "Never mind Alabama or Alaska. I want a sweet sound. Listen, this was no accident. Lucy says this, Lucy says that. You can take it from this piece of poor white trash. It has all come down. Are you listening? You have some titles I don't know about, you say them. Un Poco Loco. You know that one? Say me down. Ooooooooo, now. That's right. Ease on out of there. Oooooooooo . . ."

He lay back on the grass, keeping his arms to his side. He murmured and laughed to himself. He didn't make very much noise. Blood was all over the grass now and spreading out around him. They had finished piling up the bodies and had pulled the wagon away. It had gotten stuck in a deep split in the road and they had just walked away. A pistol shot cracked behind me. The guard in front of us stood up and looked around but he didn't seem overly anxious. He sat down against the overturned station wagon and checked the breech in his rifle. I couldn't look at what was happening next to me. He wasn't doing anything that I had to pay attention to but the blood was beginning to freak me. I had to move a few feet away. The move brought me closer to Helena. I had forgotten about her, even to the point of not seeing her. She was still breathing, her leg bent up underneath her and her arms folded over her eyes. I needed her to be awake. I needed her to be afraid so that I could reassure her. I slapped her face and she moaned but she didn't wake up. I didn't know how to intrude on her more than that. A voice screamed from inside the ruins of the colonial house.

To my left, from the east, on the road where the red wagon had been abandoned, appeared a loose line of men and women. They were guarded by five men with fatigue hats and they walked slowly towards us. I concentrated on the pile of pebbles and glass in front of me. I needed to string a yellow rope inside the first one. I needed to remember my passport picture. The man with the handlebar mustache was dead. Helena lay on her side looking at me, although there was no focus to her gaze. The line of prisoners had passed the red wagon. There were women with the men and a few small children. Their clothes were torn and several of them were naked. They stopped outside the circle. A white haired man in a red bathrobe and heavy thonged sandals stepped up to one of the guards.

"I'll ask you one more time," he said loudly. "What is the meaning of this? You have exposed my wife and children to unspeakable horrors and all this while we are faced with a terrible tragedy. Have you people gone mad?"

The guard looked past him without expression. The man stepped closer to him and yelled:

"Answer me, you cretin. We still have rights. This is still a democracy. I'll prosecute your ass out of this entire state. I demand to know your name."

"Arthur," the guard replied quietly. Then he hit him on the side of the head with the butt of his rifle. The man pitched forward across the yellow rope. A guard lifted his feet up and dumped him inside the circle. I recognized Orville. He was walking up to the circle dragging his shotgun by the barrel. He seemed distraught. He walked up to the circle and addressed the prisoners.

"All right," he said. He was unable to look at them directly. "Give me your attention now. You people are being held in custody until this day gets sorted out. Don't complain and for god's sake don't try to run away. For various reasons you are all under arrest. You will be informed of your rights later. But for now you have no rights until the city is under control. Now remove your clothes and step inside the yellow rope there."

An old woman sank to the ground. Several men stood with their arms folded, refusing to remove their clothes.

"I won't tolerate this," Orville screamed. He lifted up his shotgun. "Anyone not undressed in two minutes will be shot. Now please, do as I say."

They undressed. The women held their hands over their pubic areas. The men were less shy but

75

felt compelled to make jokes about their flabby stomachs and pale complexions. I lay back and shut my eyes. I could hear them crowding into the center of the circle, trying to avoid the bodies piled near the rope. They milled about looking for a place to sit. I felt far away, closer to the dead body next to me, and unable to say anything or even look at them. A child cried and others joined in. Their mothers tried to hush them but gave up as the crying grew louder. There was a tap on my shoulder.

"Do you know what's happening in here?" a man's voice asked. "Why have we been singled out rather than others? You've been here for a while. You saw us come in, didn't you?"

"I saw you," I said.

I heard him settle down beside me. "How come you don't open your eyes? Are you OK? What're you, traumatized?"

"I'm resting," I said. "It's been a hard day."

"Jesus Christ," he said. "I just asked. Listen, there are more of us than there are of them and we could maybe overrun them or something."

I didn't answer.

"Did you hear what I said?" he asked. "Huh?"

"I heard you," I said.

"Then why don't you respond? What are you, wounded? If you're wounded just say so. That's all. But we got to pull together, do you know what I mean? Huh? I *said* do you know what I mean?"

"Fuck off," I said.

"Whew," he said. "They really got to you, didn't they? You won't make it, mister. I'll tell you that. And I don't give a shit either."

He waited for a moment and then he moved away. I could hear shouts and the grinding of a large machine. Get me outside, I thought. Just let me stand outside and guard these people. I'll shoot their limbs off one by one if they make a false move. I'll hunt around and find more victims to put inside the circle. I'll wear a fatigue cap and swear allegiance to a fucking softball team. . . . I wanted to join up, that was all. The crowd had settled down and the children had stopped crying. I could even hear a bird chirping somewhere on the grass. There was a tap on the back of my head.

"They want you to take off your clothes." It was a girl's voice. I opened my eyes. She had long blond hair and a smooth oval face, the kind you see in hair spray or toothpaste ads. Her nipples brushed against my chest. I put one hand on her thigh and sat up.

"How long have you been here?" she asked. She sat back and put her arms around her legs.

I didn't reply.

"I think they'll let us go, don't you?" she asked. "As soon as there are no more aftershocks they'll let us go."

I stood up and took off my clothes. The girl looked me over.

"Do I suit you?"

"Oh sure," she said. "Why not?"

The guard gestured at me with his rifle to come over. I walked to the edge of the circle.

"Get that broad undressed," he said. He pointed to Helena.

"She's unconscious," I said. "Her leg is broken and she's probably fucked up in the head."

"It doesn't matter. Get her bare assed."

"Who are you guys, anyway?" I asked.

"We're a national outfit. We've been training for years for something like this."

"Yeah, but who are you?"

"Neighborhood people. We're sanctioned. You don't have to worry about it. The ALPCS."

He turned away. Another guard was walking clockwise around the circle, his rifle on his shoulder. I walked back to Helena. The girl with the blond hair remained in the same position. She watched me, her mouth slightly open. I bent over Helena, removing her sequined blue dancing slippers. Helena's eyes were open, but she was staring off to the side at the pile of dead bodies. She didn't move when I touched her.

"I have to take off your clothes," I said. "They want us bare assed. It makes us more submissive."

I unzipped her orange leotards. A bone had punctured her skin above her knee cap and I couldn't slide her leotards down more than a foot. She wasn't wearing panties and her pubic hair had been shaved. There was a soft roll of fat around her stomach.

"Is she your wife?" the girl asked.

"She was trapped in a building. We got out together."

"She doesn't look too bad for someone her age," the girl said.

"She used to be an actress."

"Oh wow," the girl said. "I think I've seen her. There was one with Natalie Wood she was in. And then she played this neurotic nurse who was trying to marry this doctor and when the leading lady ran off with him she jumped in front of a subway. Only she lived."

I leaned against Helena's leg while trying to remove her white sweater. She screamed. I tried to comfort her but she had passed out. A few people looked over at us.

"I need your help," I said. The girl crawled over and together we removed Helena's sweater. She wore no bra and there were scars around the bottom of her breast where she might have been operated on.

"Did you fuck her?" the girl asked.

"I didn't have time," I said.

"Would you make it with her if you could? I mean, say there was this little cabin right now on the beach and no one else was around. Would you get it on with her?"

"Yeah, sure," I said. Helena's face was

misshapen from pain. She looked grotesque.

"I'd do it," the girl said very quickly. "I'd make it with both of you. At the same time. And I'd take speed while I did it and then I'd come back for more. What d'you think of that?"

"I think that's fantastic."

She was leaning back against the man with the handlebar mustache. Part of her ass was resting in his dark blood. His arms were flung out to the side and his head was snapped back on the grass so that it seemed he was staring open mouthed at the blue sky. She was crying quietly, her hands playing with a piece of glass.

"I'm freaking out," she said. "I'm scared shitless if you want to know and I want to fuck someone so bad it's driving me crazy. I'm seventeen and I've made it enough to know what it does to me. I want to get out of all this. I don't want to know about any of it. I don't know how to deal with it. I was at my girl friend's house and something fell on her head and killed her. I think it was a bookcase. I ran outside and fell in with two weird guys. They were running off to blow up some TV station or something. They got killed. That's how come I'm here."

I touched her hand but she shrank back.

"Don't touch me," she snarled. "I don't want anyone touching me."

I stood up and walked counter-clockwise around the inside of the circle. As I passed the guard walking the opposite way we nodded to each other. Perhaps in some way I was guarding him as well. I stepped on glass and the bottom of my foot bled. The pain helped me concentrate on each step. I walked around the pile of bodies. An old man lay spread-eagled over the pile and a toeless foot stuck straight up between the stiff legs of three women. The line of smoke from the Hollywood Hills had thickened and spread to the east. To the south a machine gun opened up and then abruptly stopped. I took a leak over the rope. The guard paused and smiled at me.

"Some mess, ain't it?"

"It is." He had long curly brown hair and wore blue overalls and army combat boots. He had squashed up his new fatigue hat, turning the brim up at the sides to make it look old and weathered.

"You from around here?" he asked.

"I was staying at a motel on Santa Monica. They grabbed me coming out of a building. Me and some others were trying to rescue people stuck in there."

"That might be," he said seriously. "Of course we've had some godawful problems with hard hat rescue workers. They killed more than thirty of us when we moved into this area. One of them lobbed a grenade into one of our trucks. No need for that. We could have worked it out."

"Most of these people were rousted out of their homes and just marched over here and put through a bad scene."

"Yeah, it was hard for me too. I woke up on

the eighth floor and the whole goddamn building was coming down underneath me. I stood in the middle of the floor and went down with it. I just kept light-stepping it all the way down. I had to pay attention, you know what I mean?"

He walked on. I passed him again but he didn't nod. The girl had begun to walk clockwise around the circle, twenty or thirty feet behind the other guard. I was walking against them, face to face. If we had shifted our positions and moved a little differently we might have imitated the orbits of the sun and moon. A small boy stood in the middle of the circle, spinning as fast as he could until he dropped. Two other children imitated him, whirling and holding their arms straight out. "Unnhhh...Unnnhhh..." The sounds came from my stomach. I stretched and moved my neck around. The girl passed me, swinging her arms easily and smiling. An old man wobbled towards the line. He had a round pot belly and flabby testicles that hung down in loose sacs. There was a stiff curious tilt to his bald head. He made his way up to the rope and grabbed it with one hand. With the other he waved us on.

"Soooooeeeee," he cried. "Round em up. Round em up."

He walked beside me, talking to himself and slapping his hands together. When the girl passed us he moved away and began a smaller circle further in towards the center. He walked around the man with the handlebar mustache and Helena and the two bound bodies. I was getting tired. The walk wasn't working. The old man's legs suddenly buckled and he fell, landing near Helena. The guard stopped walking and lit a cigarette. The girl changed her direction and fell in alongside me.

"This is terriffic walking around like this," she said. "It does a funny thing to me. All the guards look at me wanting to jump me and you make dirty signs at me. I don't mind."

I changed my direction but she turned as well so I turned back again. I tried to growl but what came out was a low moan.

"Are you all right?" she asked.

"Get ready," I said.

She reached out with her fingers and grasped my wrist. Our fingers locked and she skipped to synchronize her steps with mine.

"You think I'm young, don't you?" she asked.

"No."

"I am. I'm just young enough to be totally wiped out and just old enough to be hysterical. But the fact that I can say that is far out, don't you think? Get ready for what?"

"Get ready to die."

It sounded completely false. I didn't know what that meant with her and neither, of course, did she. I said it again but I felt nothing. We walked in silence. She withdrew her hand from mine and after a few steps reached back again. With my other hand I let the rope run through my fingers.

"That's your trip," she said. "I'm not going to get into that one."

"Everything's going to work out," I said. "Don't worry about it."

We walked back to the center of the circle and sat down. She told me about her brother who had two fingers cut off with an axe and went to college in Oregon where he was engaged to a girl from Ohio. Her mother and father lived in Santa Barbara and ran a surfboard and skin diving business. Her great aunt had killed a prowler with a shot gun. She was afraid of heights but grooved on organic food and rock festivals. I started to tell her that I had been pointing for a disaster like this for a long time and that I recognized a lot of what was around me, but I stopped and let out a long sigh: "Waaaaaa . . ." I started to shake and she stood up and walked over to the rope. Orville was walking up the road. He stopped at the overturned station wagon and waved at the other girls to come over. The girl returned and put her hand in mine and asked me some questions:

"Do you go to movies?"

"Yes."

"Do you listen to music?"

"On the radio."

"Do you have friends?"

"In passing."

"Do you have a girl friend or a wife?"

"No."

"Have you had one lately?"

"About six months ago I stayed with a woman for a while."

"Did you like it?"

"Yes and no."

"What do you do all day?"

"Wait mostly."

"For what?"

"I don't know."

We walked over to the edge of the circle. Orville paced from the overturned station wagon to the rope. The guards had taken up positions around us. Finally Orville stopped and addressed us:

"We've found it necessary to move you to another place. There will be other groups joining you. We're going to walk down this street and get on the Freeway. We're going to take it very slowly. If we don't make the Freeway we'll do it some other way. We have three miles to walk. It will be all right if you wear your shoes but that's all."

After a few whispered words with the guards, he walked back down the road. Everyone stood up and sorted through the shoes after they were thrown over the rope. The shoes made people shrink inside themselves, as if they had been made even more naked and exposed. A fat blond woman with curlers in her hair sat down and cried. Then she beat her fists on the grass. Her husband tried to bend down and put his arms around her but she shrugged him off. "It's your fault," she screamed. "You and your weird friends." He walked off to the other side of the circle. The guards smoked and ate candy bars and checked their rifles. I found my sandals and put them on. The girl linked her arm through mine. She was wearing sandals.

"What about that woman who broke her leg?" she asked.

Helena lay on her back. Her eyes were closed.

"She'll get left behind," the girl said.

"She can't walk. It's probably better to leave her. She'll never make it otherwise."

"They'll kill her." The girl withdrew her arm and walked away. She stood next to the rope with her back to me. Helena had opened her eyes. I walked over to her and kneeled down. Her lips moved but I couldn't hear. I pressed closer.

"Water," she whispered.

"We don't have any," I said.

"I have to take a leak."

Urine squirted out of her and dribbled down her leg.

"Get me moved," she said. "I can feel the car around me. I can feel the wreck. Who's coming to get me? My leg is hurting like crazy. Don't panic. I'm all right. I'm going to get away after this."

Her words ran together and then they stopped. She closed her eyes. I walked to the edge of the circle and motioned to a guard.

"There's a lady over there who can't make it," I said. "Her leg is broken."

"Leave her," the guard said. "We'll find something to do with her."

They took down the rope and we stood patiently, waiting for a direction. A guard shouted for attention:

"All right now. I want a line. Two by two. I don't care who you pair up with but do it fast. Keep it close and don't get any ideas about going for a stroll. We got about three miles and we're going to do it as fast as we can. All right, form up."

The girl took my hand and we moved into the middle of the line. Then we all marched away. We passed the overturned station wagon and turned down a small side street. The middle of the street was torn and ripped apart and we kept to lawns as much as possible. Most of the houses were down but a few stood completely untouched. We saw no one. It was very quiet walking down the side street. A middle-aged couple whispered angrily to each other in front of us. They were suntanned and lean and walked very easily. He wanted to make a run for it but she was for staying in the line. She told him that he should try it alone, that it would be a relief to be away from him. He slapped her, not missing a step, and she turned her head away, sobbing and calling him an indulgent mother fucker. He told her that she was rotten spoiled and that she had no identity of her own and that she had bored the shit out of him for the past five years. She told him that was all right with her because she had been balling Bert for the last two years. They walked on in sullen silence.

We passed two men standing in front of the ruins of a large shopping center. They wore pistols and fatigue hats and were eating apples. One of them called out to the guard leading us:

"They're drifting in from the east now. They crossed over La Brea and are dug in near Sierra Bonita. Watch out for helicopters. They got a few of their own. God knows who's supplying them. It might be that group from up in the valley. Congressman-what's-his-face?"

They threw a few apples to the guards as we passed. An old couple in front weaved in and out of the line. A guard poked them with the butt of his rifle and they stumbled and fell. They lay in each other's arms, the old man cradling his wife's head.

"You want money?" he screamed. "You pay the fucking gas bill. We got nothing. Nothing. Why us? I ain't been two blocks either way from my house in ten years. I didn't know those people. They just come in and set up their radios. You want to shoot us, go ahead. I ask you. Do me a favor. Right between the eyes."

We walked on, leaving them behind. The side of the road was completely devastated and we had to crawl over trees and work ourselves around deep cracks that sometimes stretched for a hundred yards. We passed bodies, some of them burned beyond recognition. Four men had been hanged with clothes lines from a sagging telephone pole. We walked past the remains of small expensive

88

shops. Brightly colored clothes lay scattered on the street among paper back books and bronze bathroom fixtures. The chop-chop of a helicopter approached from the east. We dove for cover, crouching behind a pile of twisted metal outside of an antique shop. The helicopter skimmed towards us a few feet off the ground. As its shadow swept over us it suddenly shifted straight up and we felt the wind from the blades and then there was a hail of machine gun bullets. A guard fell in front of us. The other guards fired back. The man who had walked ahead of us sprang out from behind a pile of bricks and garbage cans and ran down the street. A bullet struck a stone at his feet and ricocheted off into a flower shop. He stopped and looked back at us and a guard shot him through the stomach. The helicopter whirled over us once more and then flew off, towards the south. One of the guards had been shot through the leg and two of the prisoners had been killed. There were four guards and sixteen prisoners left. The girl had curled up into a fetus position. I pulled her to her feet. The guards treated the wounded man, propping him up next to a street light and bandaging his leg. Then they formed around us again and we moved out. The wife of the man who had been shot walked by us towards the head of the line. Her eyes were glazed and she carried a pencil sharpener in her hands. She walked up to a guard and handed him the pencil sharpener. He smiled at her and she walked back to her position in the line. Ahead of us we could see the twisted shape of the Freeway. A man in the middle of the line shouted:

"If you want a three-day pass?"

He waited for a minute and then shouted out the rest:

"You got to kiss the first sergeant's ass. Hup, tuop, treep, foup; yer left, yer right, yer left, yer right, yer left."

His voice trailed off. We walked on. It was mid-afternoon and the day was clear and hot. No one spoke. The road was flooded by a broken water main and we splashed through in a foot of water. Two bodies drifted by face down until they were spun around and stopped by a truck tire. We rested at an intersection three hundred yards in front of the Freeway. Two of the guards stepped through the smashed plate glass window of a grocery store, returning with oranges, bananas, jars of caviar and boxes of cookies. They dropped them in front of us.

"A fifteen minute break," a guard said. "But don't get too comfortable."

We sagged to the ground, reaching out numbly for food. The intersection and the surrounding neighborhood had been untouched by the earthquake. Even the street lights were still standing erect. The two streets that crossed each other were small side streets composed of one story yellow stucco homes. I finished a cookie and stood up. I walked to the corner.

A guard wanted to know where I was going.

"Nowhere," I said. "I won't go away from the intersection."

He didn't reply.

I stood for a moment on the southwest corner. The prisoners sat in the middle of the intersection with the guards loosely around them. I walked to the southeast corner and then to the northeast corner. At each corner I pivoted and made a slow turn. No one was interested in me as long as I didn't move further away. I was exhausted and my ankle throbbed but I felt compelled to walk around the square. It took twelve to fourteen steps to cross each street. I wasn't interested in looking at anything. I kept walking. I made another turn and pivot. My steps were taking care of themselves. I was unable to think. I had a chance to say something to myself but it was too late for that. I had been severed from all that. I kept walking. It occurred to me briefly that I might be able to fade out altogether. If I walked calmly enough, with enough measured precision, I might become anonymous. But two teenage-blacks didn't think so. They were sitting on a lawn staring at me as I passed.

"What you people doin?" one of them asked. He was dressed in blue and white bermuda shorts and a red tee shirt. The other one, smaller and blacker, wore tuxedo pants cut off at the knees and a white buttondown shirt. They wore their afros straight out.

"Hey," said the one in the tuxedo pants. "Don't you know we been in the biggest earthquake in the history of the universe?"

I kept walking, making my turn away from them.

"Sheeeet," one of them said. "These people are all gone crazy. Everyone else has left. Out of the city. Lookit that swingin dick there. Moving around ass naked like he don't know."

The guards watched them casually. I kept my eyes to the ground and took my turn and the blacks were in front of me again.

"They is jiving," said the one in the tuxedo pants. "They taking them ownselves prisoners."

"That's some kind of misdemeanor right there," said the one in the bermuda shorts.

"You figure they don't know what's goin down in this neighborhood?"

"Trouble behind," said the one in the bermuda shorts.

"You best know it," said the one in the tuxedo pants.

A guard walked up to them. But they disappeared into the house. The guard stood on the lawn, his rifle held ready. I made my turn and the house was behind me. The other prisoners and guards were still stretched out in the middle of the intersection. I turned again and was half way across the street when a grenade was tossed through a window of the house. The explosion knocked me off my feet and I was out for a few minutes. When I came to, there was a roaring in my ears and my nose was bleeding. A piece of shrapnel had lodged into my shoulder. But nothing was broken. The guards were firing at the house, pouring in volley after volley. They began to stalk the house. Two crouched behind a tree and fired as another crawled forward a few feet. There was no answering fire. A guard rushed the door, kicking it in and spraying the inside with bullets. No one was home. Three prisoners, two women and a man, ran across the intersection and down the street, in the opposite direction of the house. They swayed and stumbled, gasping for breath. The guard behind the tree watched them and then the others came out of the house and stood watching. One of the women fell. She was small and flat chested and she cried out when she hit the sidewalk. The man turned back for her but the other woman kept going, disappearing behind a garage. A guard squeezed off a shot at the woman on the sidewalk. She was in the act of standing when the bullet smashed through her back. She pitched forward across the man, who was running towards her. He crawled away from her, his feet slipping out from underneath him. He was short and fat and had a hard time crawling. He stopped and stood up, his hands over his head. Three of the guards fired at once and the bullets lifted him backwards off his feet. The guards walked towards us. An old woman began to moan.

"All right," a guard said. "All right." He was large and his khaki pants and shirt hung loosely over him. Sweat poured down his beefy face and he had lost his fatigue cap. He squinted at us angrily, then yelled out:

"Which one of you dick sucking creeps is going to make a break for it? I seen enough of you people for one day. Give me one ass licking chance and I'll take care of that problem."

My shoulder was bleeding and I could feel the shrapnel next to the bone. The girl was holding hands with a short man with long black hair and black cowboys boots and I was left at the end of the line. There was a small aftershock and we kneeled on the street until it passed. Then we walked on. The street was quiet. A guard walked beside me, his rifle smoking. He looked like he was having trouble keeping himself together. His fat lips trembled and his smooth blue eyed face had been blackened and badly bruised. He handed me a handkerchief and I tried to stop up the blood in my shoulder. It didn't help.

"How far we got to go?" I asked him.

"Less than a mile." I could tell he wanted to talk. "What'd they get you for?" he asked.

"Maybe breaking and entering," I said. "I don't know. I was in a building and when I came out they grabbed me. I don't know what's happening. I don't know who you guys are."

"They've made a lot of mistakes," he admitted. "But it's hard not to in a situation like this.

We can't take chances. There are a lot of bad willed people trying to take over and the country won't have a chance if they do. You must know about it. Everyone knew this was going to happen. We've been preparing for this ever since the last quake, back in '70."

I didn't answer. The smoke from the west was growing thicker and it was becoming hard to breathe.

"My wife and two kids got killed." He didn't look at me as he spoke. "I ran outside to see what had happened and when I turned around half the house and the carport was gone. I could hear my littlest girl, Lois, crying but I couldn't get to her. I was digging with my hands but I couldn't do anything. I couldn't get anyone to help me. They had their own problems. I just sat there and waited until I couldn't hear anything. Then I reported to my station. If I didn't have this to do I would probably be dead or crazy by now."

He stared at the ground and I kept my eyes on the back of the man in front of me. After a while he spoke again:

"You know that guy that got killed by the grenade? Well, he was a high school basketball coach. His team was going to play for the Class B Championship this Saturday. He used to play guard for USC. All-Conference. He once sank nine straight jump shots outside the key against Kentucky."

His steps faded behind me.

"Goddamn spades," I heard him say to himself. "I should have shot them. Nobody figured on them. Not around here anyway. Baker company was supposed to have taken care of them. Well, fuck Baker company. Holbrook, that's who it is. Holbrook's responsible. Stupid asshole. I never liked him. Always bullshitting and knowing everything. His wife knows it all too. He'll run for some office. I won't back him. Hell, I might even blow off his goddamn head. . . ."

He mumbled on. We were approaching the Freeway. The overpass had sagged and there was a large crack running down the middle. A lot of the Freeway had fallen in. We waited at the foot of the ramp while a guard scouted ahead. The other guards sat with their rifles between their legs, eating candy bars. They no longer bothered to watch us closely. No one had the strength or desire to make a run for it. A fire engine had overturned and lay smashed against one of the pilings of the Freeway. The girl lay against one wheel, her legs spread apart and one hand inside her cunt. She stared at the sky with lost vacant eyes. The man with the black cowboy boots sat beside her, rubbing his feet and making faces at the ground. My shoulder had stopped bleeding but I kept the handkerchief pressed to the wound. The guard that had scouted ahead waved us on and we made our way up the ramp. From the Freeway we could see smoke covering the west and north and small fires scattered throughout the city. I stared without seeing, without feeling. We walked west straight down the double line on the middle of the Freeway. A tall humpbacked man in front of me jerked his head up and down and talked furiously to himself. He lurched out of line but the guards didn't seem to notice. He stuck his finger up his ass and walked straight ahead, whistling. There was firing from the south and we stopped. We crouched down as the guards crept to the side of the Freeway and peered over the cement barrier. The man with the finger up his ass walked on, moaning and stamping his feet. The firing stopped but the guards remained behind the barrier.

"We're too exposed," a guard yelled. "We'll get picked off like rabbits."

"We only got a little ways to go," yelled the florid faced guard. "We can see em coming from up here."

"No way I'm going on," said the young guard who had given me his handkerchief. "It's a shooting gallery up here."

"We're going on," shouted the florid faced guard.

"There ain't no difference," said another guard. "We might as well go on."

The florid faced guard stood up and motioned for us to move out. The young guard shook his head but he stood up and walked beside us. He was talking to himself, spitting every few feet and laughing. We had gone two hundred yards when a woman fell at the head of the line. Far ahead we could see the man with the finger up his ass break into a run and disappear down a ramp. The woman had been shot through the throat. We lay without moving.

"Silencer," said the guard with the florid face. "The fuckers got themselves a silencer. It must be cops. We got to go underneath."

"You're fucking A we got to go underneath," said the young guard. "We got to go underneath everything."

We crawled ahead to the next ramp. The young guard talked all the way:

"God help us now. They got cops on us now. They'll pick us off like rats. They've got tanks, man. Helicopters. They were always the ones. I'm not gonna make it. We ought to shoot em and get the hell out. Who are they, anyway? Make it up to the mountains. That's where we're supposed to be anyhow. Oh Mary I'm gonna throw up."

He bent over and threw up. Then he lay down on the Freeway and closed his eyes. The florid faced man crawled up to him.

"You all right, Billy?" He placed a hand on his shoulder. "You can make her, Billy. We'll put these bastards in their cages and then we'll lay back. Come on now, boy, we're gonna make it now."

"I ain't gonna make it," Billy said. "I'm coming apart from inside."

"You'll make it." His voice was insistent. "You

can't give up, Billy. You can't be a quitter. This is the most important day of your life, of any man's life. I won't let you cash it in. This day is bigger than you, bigger than all of us. It's what we've been waiting for, planning for."

Billy looked up at him. "When that quake struck it was like a big tear, like the earth was ripped open. Did you hear that sound? It was like linoleum being ripped apart."

The florid faced man slapped Billy hard on the shoulder and crawled on. Billy followed, slowly shaking his head from side to side. We made it to the head of the ramp and half crawled, half slid to the bottom. We started out again, walking slowly under the shadow of the Freeway. The street was full of fallen billboards and large chunks of neon. The day had grown cooler, despite the fires to the west. There was an increasing stench of sewage and burning bodies and there were dogs now openly sniffing at the bodies and food underneath the rubble. There was no breeze and the sky was nearly dark with smoke. We stopped abruptly, the guards motioning us to be silent. They herded us further underneath the Freeway and made us lie down. A column of men passed overhead, their voices muttering and their equipment softly squeaking. We lay silently until their sounds had faded.

"Hard hats," said a guard. "They find you and you wish you was dead. They're the new kind, teachers and the like."

"No telling who it was," said the florid faced

guard. "Could be some of our own although they was walking east. They might have delivered prisoners and be walking back."

"I wish we had us a walkie talkie or a loud speaker or something to yell through," said another guard. "We got to get ourselves on the air, *any* air." He squatted down and lit a cigarette. His mouth was caked with blood and three of his upper teeth were missing. "I don't feel too good without communications. You can't tell who you are or what you're doing without communications."

Billy took out a worn deck of cards from his pocket. He spread them out in front of him and began to play solitaire.

"I'm going to have me a picnic," he said to himself. "A few shuffles for my own pleasure and then some eats. I ain't going nowhere. I been walking backwards. You say I'm going somewhere but I ain't."

The florid faced man took a step towards him and then shrugged and turned away. A small gnome-like man stepped from one of the cracked pillars that supported the Freeway. He walked confidently towards us, unconcerned that the guards had lifted their rifles towards him. He wore two raincoats, one white and one black, and carried a bulging suitcase. He threw his suitcase in front of Billy and sat down. The guards lowered their rifles.

"I bring no false moves," he said to Billy. "I could be your father as like as anyone else. How many are you, boy?"

"I don't know," Billy said. "Thousands most likely. We're scattered all over the place."

The gnome-like man scooped up the cards and cut the deck with one hand. "What are we playin for?" he asked.

"I got nothin," Billy said.

"Come on now," he said, dealing the cards. "You got to play for something or you don't get nothing back. You can't sit here in the middle of all this and jerk yourself off."

"I'll play for my weapon here."

"No good."

"I'll throw in my clothes."

"Nothing to that," the man said. "Goods don't mean nothing anymore. This suitcase isn't worth a fucking thing. I'll play you for your services. I win and you come my way. You win and I'll help you along your way. Straight draw."

"I ain't got no way, mister," Billy said. "Besides that you're bottom dealing me."

"You seen that, did you?" He laid out three aces to Billy's two pairs.

"I seen it," Billy said. "And I welcome it. I ain't going nowhere."

"I know you aren't, son," the gnome-like man said. "And as soon as these others move on we'll open us up the suitcase and have us a time."

"You want to shake on it?" Billy asked.

"Hell, no." He began to rub his forehead with both hands. "We ain't got nothing to shake on. That's the beauty of it."

"That's right," Billy shouted. "That's purely right." He whispered in the other's ear and they both laughed.

The florid faced man walked over to Billy. "You comin?" he asked.

"I'm falling out," Billy giggled. "I got me a new partner and we're going to do a different kind of prospecting."

"I ought to shoot you both," the florid faced man said.

"You'd be doing us a favor," said the gnome-like man.

"Ah fuck you both." The florid faced man turned towards us and motioned for us to move on. We left Billy sitting in front of the gnome-like man, laughing and slapping the ground in front of him. No one looked back.

We walked over giant letters from a theater marquee. All around us were signs of a battle. Two men hung over the windowsill of a pool emporium, their backs shredded with bullet holes. Empty shell casings lay scattered everywhere. We were climbing across broken tables and piles of rotting fruit when a voice shouted for us to halt. We sank to the ground.

"Name yourself," a voice demanded.

"ALPCS with prisoners."

"San Diego Chargers," the voice said.

"Ring twice."

"You're on."

We were told to stand. We picked our way through the rubble to where three men in fatigue hats held rifles on a dozen men. They were Mexicans and several were wounded. They wore khaki pants and cheap sport shirts and two of them wore brown berets.

"We thought you was dead," said one of the men guarding the Mexicans. He was tall, with a thin white mustache and bright blue eyes. He wore a red ribbon in the middle of his fatigue cap. "Hammiker told us you were either lost or the desert guerrillas got you. We heard they were starting to move in. Say, you got them bare assed. Now ain't that a treat."

"We had a hell of a time getting this far," said the florid faced guard.

They moved off a few feet and talked together. There were three groups now and they formed a rough triangle. The guards stood to the south, drinking beer and cleaning their rifles. The Mexicans stood huddled to the north. The rest of sprawled at the apex, to the east. The girl came up to me and smiled.

"I feel very teensy weensy," she said. "Like a cigarette butt lost in a big ashtray." She spoke in a little girl's voice. "Where are we going?" she asked. When I didn't answer she asked me again.

"We're going to a concrete block house surrounded by dead elm trees and beyond that a huge swamp."

"What will we do there?" she asked.

"We'll eat a big meal and watch TV."

"What will we eat?"

She was rubbing her cunt. The man with the black cowboy boots came up and held her other hand. He rolled a broken milk bottle back and forth with his foot and stared off to the north, past the Mexicans.

"Egg rolls," said the man with the black cowboy boots. "Then pigs' knuckles, pickles, cheeseburgers and blintzes."

"What will we do after we eat?" she asked.

"I don't know," I said.

"We'll row out in the swamp and shoot alligators and water lilies," said the man with the black cowboy boots.

"That will be nice," she said.

The guard with the red ribbon walked over to the Mexicans, snapping a stick against his thigh. Two guards walked behind him.

"You spicks get undressed and line up with the rest of them faggots," he said.

After the Mexicans had undressed we were lined up in pairs. The girl and the man with the black cowboy boots were further up the line and I was paired off with a large white haired woman with broken horn rimmed glasses. She looked at me steadily, moving her tongue over her lips and nodding, as if in affirmation. We moved out past the remains of a brick church and over the smashed

104

kaleidoscope colors of stained glass. We walked in silence. Ahead of us a large red cloth with a white line running through it had been nailed to a tree. Underneath the tree sat half a dozen men with fatigue hats. A yellow school bus was parked in front of them. As we approached the bus we saw men and women inside, sitting in the seats and standing in the aisles. The door was closed and a guard sat on the step outside, a rifle across his lap. We stopped fifty feet away from the flag, while the man with the red ribbon talked to the guards. He spread a map over the fender of the bus and after they had looked at it he folded it and walked back to us. A guard opened the door of the bus and told everyone to get out and take off their clothes. They were young and unusually pale. Tiny silver crucifixes hung from their necks, and their hair, including the women's, was cropped short. A woman stumbled and a guard struck her with the butt of his rifle. She smiled at him. They crowded in among us, smiling and nodding and telling each other how good it was to stretch their legs. Then we moved out again. We walked three more blocks and turned west, away from the Freeway. Two men with fatigue hats joined us from a side street, leading three blacks bound together by a short knotted rope around their necks. They were shoved roughly into the line.

"Don't push me," said the woman next to me. "I'm going as fast as I can."

"I'm not pushing," I said. "I'm walking beside you."

"I don't care what you're doing," she said. "You're pushing. Where are they taking us?"

I told her I didn't know.

"I just hope there's food," she said. "I don't want to think about all this atrocity. They say a lot of the coast has dropped into the Pacific. I wouldn't doubt it. My husband was in on it. He knew it was coming for years. I heard him talk on the phone a few times. Mr. Bigshot here, Mr. Bigshot there. He had maps and everything. He was one of the first ones they shot. I never thought he had it in him. All I had yesterday was a hamburger. I had two Pepsis this morning. That's all."

We turned a corner and walked past small factories and warehouses. Two blocks ahead of us a group of men in fatigue hats sat near the remains of a red brick high school. A small concrete stadium stood to the right of the high school. There was a long shiver through the line and then a soft whimpering sigh. We were prodded through a gate and onto a football field. The afternoon sun was beginning to slide towards the smoke filled horizon and hazy shadows streaked across the field. Perhaps it was Saturday. I remembered it was fall. More than fifty naked men and women sat on the field. Some were wounded and dying. A deep crevice ran in a jagged line across the center of the field. The stands faced us on the west, with smoke rising up behind them. The seats were thirty rows deep and sections had fallen in at both ends but the center sections were still intact. Guards sat and slept in the stands and stood in groups around the south end of the field. The goal posts on the south side were still standing. I sat down on the forty-five yard line and faced them. I only existed. And yet I still had the evening and night and what lay beyond to get through. My eyes recorded what was in front of me but only as a reflex, a habit that no longer mattered. A few men and women wandered among the prisoners, looking for relatives or someone they recognized. But there were no recognitions, no news, no information. I had lost sight of the girl. I walked towards the eastern side of the field, looking for her. I stepped over the sideline but was waved back by a guard. We had been restricted to the field. I walked along the northern side of the crevice. It was two feet across at its widest and seemed to have no bottom. The girl was not around. I walked towards the middle of the field looking for a place where I could jump across. A few bodies had fallen into the crevice or lay at the edge. Most of them were dead although a few hung about as if wanting to make the plunge. The crevice narrowed and I stepped across. A hand reached up for me but I danced away like a broken field runner. Then my ankle gave out and I tripped. I lay on my stomach, barely able to breathe. Two men lay beside me, their eyes open, their cheeks pressed to the grass. We looked at each other.

"I thought you was O. J. Simpson," said one of

the faces. It was a thin face with loose upper dentures and black swollen eyes. "Comin on down, then swivel hipping side steps and falling for extra yardage. You're a player, all right. I'll bet you could make it to the crack if you was to give it half a try."

"What about Jim Brown?" the other face said. Blood trickled out the side of his mouth and his long blond hair was matted with dirt and oil. "Jim Brown was a tank. He'd drag two people with him up to that crack. He didn't bother jiving and juking with the hips. He just rolled. Three steps would get him into that crack."

"That dates you," said the other. "They got new kinds of runners now. It's a new day now. Them that do 9.3 in the hundred and like to weigh over two twenty. These boys are the New Breed, you know what I mean. Corn fed and they got good medical care and nothing to overcome. Everyone's an All-American now. Hell, hundreds of em could make it into that crack and drag their tacklers along with em."

The man with the loose upper dentures squinted at me. "You trying to make it into the crack or are you running away from the crack?"

"I don't belong to any team," I said.

"A lot of people have slipped into that crack." He rolled over on his back. "I'm coming away from it myself. First two hours I was here you couldn't keep me away from it. I was very close to dropping in."

I stood up and stepped over him. He grabbed my ankle and gave it a twist and I kicked him in the face. We struggled silently and then I managed to slip away. I limped towards the goal posts, resting on the ten yard line. On the goal line a guard was about to profane a prisoner. The prisoner was not more than eighteen. He was made to kneel on the ground, his long red hair over his eyes, his fingers grabbing into the grass, his upper body shaking with sobs. The guard was short and thickly muscled through the chest, his arms covered with sinewy tattoos, his hair black and slicked down over his flat forehead. His pants had dropped to his ankles. He held a pistol to the boy's head while he worked on his cock with the other hand. His mouth slowly chewed a wad of gum and his red rimmed eyes stared off across the field. When he was finally ready, he dropped his pistol and his hands gripped the boy's thighs and he worked into him with short brutal thrusts. A few guards stood near the goal posts, watching without comment. The prisoners nearby turned away and moved to the other end of the field. The boy screamed and the cry hung over the stadium for a long moment before it died away. A man with a green ribbon on his fatigue cap walked quickly up to the guard. He was very tall and erect and his white hair and square jaw gave him a military bearing. He removed an ivory handled colt from a black leather holster around his waist. He pointed the colt at the guard and pulled back the hammer. The guard was unable to stop his orgasm, even as he saw the pistol pointed at him, and he pitched forward onto the back of the boy.

"Get up," the man behind the colt said.

The guard stood up, awkwardly pulling up his pants and trying to focus his eyes.

"I didn't mean nothing," he said. "He was making signs to me all the way down here."

The guard was slapped across the face with the barrel of the colt and half dragged towards the goal posts. A rope was called for. The boy was escorted to a position underneath the goal posts. The rope was tied around the guard's neck in a tight noose and then thrown over the cross bar. The boy was made to kneel on all fours. The guard was hoisted onto his back by three other guards and the rope drawn taut. He stood with his legs wavering, his eyes wide, his bound hands jerking for balance. He screamed and then the boy pitched forward and he was left dangling. I moved up the field. I crossed the fifteen yard line and fell forward to the twenty. My ankle had given out again and I had lost too much blood from my shoulder. I lay on my stomach, stretching out towards the thirty yard line. Three men sat with their backs to me, facing the crevice. They were talking slowly, with great effort.

"Tell you one thing more . . . this ain't just an earthquake. . . . More is at stake here. Whole state like this. Mobs. Looting. Maybe the whole country. They've set off the worst. Inhuman things. . . ."

"I don't want to be around. I'll tell you that. I ain't scared of dying now. I knew this would happen. Never did anything. Never prepared. Never could think about it."

"When I find the son-of-a-bitch that's responsible for marching me off like a convict, I'll kill him . . . I'll . . . have . . . his . . . ass. I'm no threat. . . . I was standing on my lawn watching the fire across the street. I'm gonna do more than press charges. . . ."

"They got no call . . . to hold us. . . . They haven't said what we done. Go on up and ask one of those guys with a ribbon in his hat. . . . Both my legs are broke. . . ."

"They don't listen."

I crawled past them. Some of the guards had started a fire on the western side of the field and were cooking steaks and lambchops. I crawled past the thirty and up to the thirty-five yard line. Prisoners were walking numbly towards the food, standing near the sidelines and staring at the smoking meat. The girl sat near the crevice. She was slowly bowing her head over and over again, as if she was throwing up. She looked at me without recognition.

"I met some nice people," she said.

She looked past me and smiled. I sat with her and together we stared into the crevice.

"What do you think is down there?" she asked.

"Nothing," I said.

"Oh, I think there's a lot down there. I think there's more than you know down there."

"No one knows," I said. "Why should you know? You don't have to know. You don't even have to know what's going to happen."

"I have to know," she said.

A man crawled towards the crevice. He was old and fat and his belly hung underneath him like a balloon full of water. When he reached the edge of the crevice he stopped, folding his hands underneath his head and shutting his eyes.

"Are you going to crawl in?" the girl asked.

The man didn't answer. He opened his eyes and looked sadly at her as she crawled up to the edge. I grabbed her ankle but she shrugged me off. She sat on the edge and swung her legs over. I sat beside her, swinging my own legs over but grabbing on to the grass.

"What if we're pushed from behind?" she said. "They've been pushing people in, you know. I dare you not to look back."

I didn't look back. She looked back and then giggled.

"I don't think it's so deep," she said. "Not more than a mile."

"Why don't you shut up?" said the man across the crevice.

"I'm sorry," the girl said. "I really think I'm sorry. Are you going to jump in?"

He looked at us and dangled his short legs over the edge.

"I might take a jump or I might not," he said. "I'm not even sure I'm thinking about it."

"I think you ought to jump," I said. "You're just jerking yourself off like this."

"Yeah," he said. "I don't know whether I'm a jumper or not. Ask me two days ago and I'm not a jumper. I got to think on it now."

He looked off towards the sidelines, banging his heels against the side of the crevice. The guards held the steaks and lambchops in their hands and ripped the meat apart with their teeth. Occasionally one of the guards would throw a bone to the prisoners and they would dive and fight for it. The field was becoming agitated. There was more noise and movement among the prisoners and the guards had begun to drink heavily. Three men and a woman left the sidelines and walked to the crevice. The woman and two of the men sat down on the side I was sitting on. They sat far apart, their legs over the edge and their eyes staring off across the field. The other man jumped over the crevice, jumped back again and then hopped over to the far side. He sat down, with his legs over the edge. I recognized him as the man with the black cowboy boots who had spent some time walking beside the girl. He waved at her and she smiled at him.

"I don't need that meat," he said. "It's weird how they're getting hungry over there. Couldn't eat

113

right now. Nossir. I'd throw it all up." He spoke more to himself than to her and it was hard to hear his voice. The girl swayed forward and then sideways and ran her tongue over her lips.

"Well I'm hungry," the fat man said. "I don't remember the last time I ate. I don't remember anything. I can barely remember what kind of a job I had, who my wife was, what sports my kids played, where the fuck I even used to live. You're goddamn right I'm hungry. They should throw us something. That's what this country is all about, putting stuff into you. They deny you that and you know the worst has happened. There's food lying all over the streets. We could have one of the great meals of all time."

One of the other men began to cry. Finally he stood up and walked away, towards the goal posts. The shadows had reached the other side of the field and the sun was hidden behind clouds of smoke. There were screams and shouts as the guards tossed more bones and scraps of meat onto the field.

"I'm from West Virginia," the fat man said. His eyes were locked onto the cooking meat. "They've got beer over there now. And potato chips. I don't believe this. It's a regular cook out. We got about ten seconds left and they're barbecuing the shit out of everything. I can't stand it. I'm from Wheeling, near the Ohio line."

He stood up and walked towards the sidelines. The man with the black cowboy boots lowered himself into the crevice and disappeared. The fat man walked back and forth from the forty-five to the thirty yard line. Once he fell forward in a scramble for a bone but he was too slow. All of the guards were gathered on the side of the field now except for three men with red and green ribbons on their fatigue hats who sat in the stands. The fat man stepped across the line and grabbed a lambchop from the improvised grill. He ran back into the center of the field, stuffing it into his mouth with both hands. Two more men rushed the grill and grabbed steaks. The crowd suddenly spilled across the line. A guard shot a man through the head with his pistol. The girl and I stood up and tried to run towards the goal posts. People fell near us. She stumbled and fell and I knelt by her as a black ran by with a gun, firing into the stands. There were answering shots and he was hit in the stomach and head. He fell backwards, landing in the girl's lap. She rocked him back and forth.

"You're dying," she said to him. "I can tell because all the blood is pouring out of you and I don't know how to turn off the faucet."

I placed him on the ground.

"I've met some very nice people today," she said. "And others not so nice."

A few of the prisoners had made their way to the stands and managed to find weapons. Two men were shot very quickly in front of us. Three prisoners forgot about the crevice and fell in as they

115

ran across the field. A man and a woman crawled by.

"We have nothing to lose," said the man.

"Lie here," the woman said. "Pretend we're dead."

"We're already dead," the man said. He raised her up and together they staggered across the field, flailing their arms and shouting. A woman slid across the grass and touched the girl's hand. She shrank back but the woman reached out again for her and the girl held her hand. The woman was bleeding badly from the shoulder and neck.

"Take my ring," the woman said to the girl. She tried to pull a diamond ring off her finger but she wasn't strong enough. The girl pulled it off for her and slipped it over her own finger.

"Tell Harry Stralinger that I didn't make it," the woman said. "He lives on 302 Cuesta Way. Tell him that he can go to all the Holiday Inns he wants to and that I would have gone to Acapulco with him, only not on that weekend that Robert was around. He wouldn't have survived against Robert."

She died on the grass in front of us. I raised my hand to stop the girl from standing up and a bullet went through my palm. The girl smiled.

"You won't be able to wave to me now," she said. "You'll have to use your other hand. But maybe you're left handed anyway."

She walked towards the center of the field. I sat

up and watched her cross the forty yard line. A bullet smacked into her shoulder and she spun and fell. I crawled forward and lay down beside her. She groaned but kept her eyes closed.

"I'm always pulling bodies off you," I said.

"You can shoot me," she said. "That's what you've wanted to do all along."

"We'll be all right if we don't move, " I said.

"I'm not moving. You're the one who's moving. You don't have to keep following me around."

I tried to stop her wound but there was nothing around that would serve as a bandage.

"I can't get my eyes open," she said. "Say something to me. How do I know you haven't crawled off?"

"It's a relief to know I'm not as bad off as you," I said.

"Say something else," she said.

I opened up my mouth. "Oooooooooooooo," came out.

"Oh no," she said. I could barely hear her. "No, don't do that. You're putting me on. That's like the night. Be something else."

I couldn't speak. The pain in my hand was causing me to forget where I was.

"I know. I know," she said. "But hold me anyway."

I rolled over on her, covering her with my stomach, my arms and legs. My limp cock was

117

pressed between her thighs, my bloody hand reached down to her waist. I held her and the blood gurgled up between her clenched teeth. There were pistol shots on the far side of the field as guards walked among the wounded and shot them through the head. I held her tighter, afraid that she would cry out. I even thought of strangling her, except that she was still whispering to me, pleading to be held, to be pressed into the earth. Two guards walked towards us, stopping every three or four steps to shoot a prisoner. One of them took a leak a few yards away. They talked quietly:

"There ain't hardly any left."

"I don't like shooting them. But I guess things got too far out of hand."

"We're in the middle of a no-man's-land. We're out of water now and the food will go bad and there isn't electricity and the fires are spreading."

"Time to make a move to the country."

"The roads are blocked. We got to make it here."

A shot was fired and then another. They ran downfield, towards the goal posts. We lay still, soaked in blood, hardly breathing. I might have passed out for a few minutes. A man cried for Peter and voices moaned through the stadium. Over it all a strange stillness descended as the moans became one sound, one supplication and then for a moment they stopped and there wasn't any sound at all. The girl was no longer breathing. "Ahhhhhhhhhhh," I sighed. And then my own breath gave out for a few seconds. I sucked it in and stood up. No one fired at me and I walked cautiously forward for a few yards. The wounded were rising slowly to their feet and walking aimlessly across the field. I stopped at the feet of a dead guard. His legs had been smashed, as if run over by heavy wheels. He lay on his back, his hands thrown over his face. I knelt beside him and ripped off part of his orange and blue striped shirt. There was a low hum around me, a mournful pitch that never varied. I waited to see where it was coming from but there was no location to the sound. It occurred to me that the hum was coming from inside me, that the lower to the ground I was the more involved with sound I became. I stood up and the sound diminished. I sank down again and it increased. I tied the shirt around my wounded hand, put on the guard's fatigue cap and walked across the field. There was no trouble at all going through the exit gate.

The street was full of small expensive shops and restaurants. Most of the roofs of the buildings had caved in and glass lay everywhere. I had walked a few blocks when I heard voices from inside a drugstore. A man and a woman were furiously rummaging through boxes and bottles that lay scattered over the floor. Another man was scooping out the insides of an icebox at the rear of the store. A woman stood off to the side, leaning against a

119

smashed counter, a syringe dangling between her thumb and forefinger. Her head snapped to her chest and she slumped to the floor, still managing to hold on to the syringe. She wore blue silk pajamas with a gold sash around her narrow waist and a black stiff brimmed Navaho hat over her long blond hair. I sat down inside the door. They were all dressed in outrageous outfits and I felt a sudden need to put on more clothes, to wear three or four shirts and several pairs of pants. The man investigating the icebox nodded to me and then went back to the glass vial he was holding. He poured a line of white powder onto the back of his wrist. Holding one nostril closed with his forefinger he sniffed the powder into the free nostril. He wore a gray shark skinned suit, yellow leather shoes and a large black fedora. The man searching through the rubbish on the floor was dressed in white cowboy boots and a black silk Japanese robe over a yellow stretch bathing suit. The other woman was older and white haired. She wore a man's tuxedo with a blue and white polka dot tie around her waist and white sneakers on her feet. She was preparing to shoot up.

"If you want us you'll have to take us," said the man in the fedora. He held a long surgical knife in his hand, extended towards me. His eyes were heavy lidded, his mouth open, his teeth smashed and missing.

"I don't want you," I said.

"How come you don't want us?" asked the white haired woman. "We're having a ball, aren't we, Dickie? Isn't this the best it's been all day?"

"It is," said the man in the fedora. "It's the very best."

"He's with those guys in the fatigue hats," said the man in the silk robe. "They ran by an hour ago. You're late, mister. They're probably in Pasadena by now."

"They're crazy," said the girl in the Navaho hat. "No way you're going to get me to go with them. They're out to take over the city. No way. You understand?" She lifted up her head to look at me but the effort was too much and her head slumped forward.

They turned back to their work. The man with the fedora shoved out the icebox trays and then kicked the icebox.

"Cheap bastards," he said. "Not enough to get a mouse off. We got to hit three or four more stores if we're going to last a week."

The man in the silk robe spoke softly to himself:

"There's a lot of goddamn redemption around here. I don't care what you say. You don't see too many people attached to their pain around here. Nossir."

I walked down the block and went into a shoe store. The shoe boxes had fallen from the shelves and lay all over the floor. A small man in a raincoat sat on one chair trying on a pair of moccasins. He whistled loudly and smiled at me as I came in.

"I'm going to put on a terrific stand somewhere," he said. "They might be berserk all around me but my wardrobe is going to shine. *Shine,* that's spelt with an S."

I put on a few pairs of shoes but then decided I would go with my sandals. The decision left both of us giggling and exhausted. I left him huddled over a pair of white bucks. I walked down the street, keeping next to the edge of the buildings. I had lost blood and was unable to walk without becoming dizzy. And yet I was hungry. There was a restaurant across the street. It was a Hamburger Hamlet with half of a red awning still intact. The door was caved in and I had to enter through the window. It was very dark. I lay for a while on the rug. The ceiling had sagged to within four feet of the floor and I had to crawl. I crawled past the bar and a row of booths with leather seats. There were candles on the floor. I picked one up and looked for a match. I had to crawl behind the bar before I found one. I lit the candle and crawled forward. I finally found the kitchen. The ceiling was high enough for me to stand. I walked over to the freezer. The meat was still unspoiled. I picked up a roast and bit into it. I grabbed apples and potato chips and pickles and sat down on the floor and ate it all. Then I went back for more. I ate until I couldn't move. I slept for a while and was woken up by a laugh from the dining room. I picked up a kitchen knife and blew out the candle.

"I know you're in there, baby," a voice said. "I saw your little light."

I didn't answer.

"Where did you find matches?" he asked. "You ain't keeping all that food for yourself, are you? That would go down as hoarding.""

I still didn't answer.

"I can always go to another place but I ain't going to. That's how relentless I am. I love Hanburger Hamlets. I met my first wife in one. So if you don't slide out of there or tell me who you are or make some kind of a sociable sign, I'm coming in."

I stood up and howled. I threw glasses against the wall and broke plates and bowls. Then I sat down. My heart was pounding and I had trouble breathing. I lit a candle but then snuffed it out. I grabbed the knife and tried to creep forward but my arm buckled underneath me. I lay on the floor for a while. He was making no sound but I didn't believe he had left. I started out again. I certainly wanted to kill him, or at least somebody. The desire pushed me forward, my ass sticking up in the air and my head bent hopelessly forward. I finally made it into the dining room. Further down, in one of the booths, a man sat behind the soft glow of a candle. His head grazed the ceiling and one hand encircled a broken champagne bottle. I moved forward another few feet.

"I got you fixed very clearly, old buddy," he said softly. "I'm just sitting here drinking champagne and waiting for you to clear out of the kitchen so I can get me a taste of that good food."

"How are you doing?" I asked.

"Just fine," he said. "Just very fine. But you don't look too good."

"I'm real good," I said. "I couldn't be better."

"I figure you snapped," he said. "Just by the way you screamed your ass off and the way you're crawling in here. I been into a little killing myself today. I understand it. It keeps the motor going. It's hard to stop once you get into it. But I figured as long as I was in here and it getting dark and all we could guard this place and stock pile some food. Because it's going to get very hairy from here on in, you know what I mean?"

"I know what you mean." He took a drink from the bottle and wiped his mouth with the back of his hand. The light was too dim for me to see his face clearly.

"But you got to know I'm getting into that kitchen one way or the other. War or peace, you understand. But you sure look far worse off than me. I had it easy most of the day. Hid out. I even got a few hours' sleep. How's that for sustaining your cool? Huh? I could do twenty push ups and a couple of back flips right now. I been working out regularly and I swim and bowl every weekend. You don't even like look like you're going to make it through the next few hours, let alone the night. Too much of a heavy taste today. Right, buddy?"

"I'm all right," I said.

He took another drink and blew out the candle. He chuckled and I could hear him slide off the booth.

"I'm coming for you know, sweet baby," he whispered softly. "And I got me a big broken bottle to play with."

I slid off to the side. I couldn't see or hear anything. I slowly climbed onto a booth and then slid up on the table. There wasn't anything to do but wait. But as much as I was passive I wanted to plunge the knife into him. I wanted the knife to go through him and out the other side. I focused on the pain in my hand and it helped me to pay attention. I was definitely coming unwrapped. I wanted to kill him so badly. I was certainly going to deny him food. I was going to deny him air if I could. He suddenly loomed up from the rug and came straight on. I held the knife in front of me with both hands and he plunged onto it, as if that is what he had wanted all along. The broken bottle scraped my shoulder and neck and he tried to swing it back into me but he was already dying. The knife went in up to the hilt. It felt very good. He coughed and sighed and I retained and treasured the sigh because it was his very last. Warm urine ran down my leg. It was a long time before I was able to move. I lay with him on top of me, still holding the knife. Finally I slid to the floor and crept towards the door. I sniffed and tried to moisten my dry lips with my tongue. When I found the smashed window I was ready to kill again. "Oooooooo," I said out loud and the sound comforted me. But when I looked outside even though the street was empty, I shrank back into the darkness of the restaurant. I was shaking and I needed other steps as well as my own. A woman helped me. She was weaving down the middle of the street clutching a doorknob, wearing only a fireman's hat and galoshes. She was middle-aged and plump and she was covered with blood. I could hear her laugh and talk to herself, the words running into themselves so that it sounded as if she was talking in tongues. Slowly she executed a series of figure eights from one side of the street to the other. She stared at me, slapping her thighs and shouting unknown words and as I stepped further out into the street she turned faster and faster. The late afternoon light was soft and diffuse through the heavy layers of smoke. I began my own turn further down the street, turning slowly at first but then going faster. We shouted and whirled and flung our arms over our heads and my fear receded and I was able to stop. After the dizziness had left me I looked towards her. She lay crumpled in a heap, her stubby legs bent underneath her, one arm twisted and grotesquely extended at a right angle. I knew she was dead. I lay on my back, staring at the sky. The sky was no help. There were steps coming at me

126

from down the street. There was a hub cap lying next to me and I put it over my face. I needed to hide. My eyes couldn't take any more. The steps came closer and they seemed to belong to a dozen or so men and women. They sat down around me.

"If you don't keep up, we're going to leave you," said a man's voice.

A woman answered, her voice weary and disgusted. "Go ahead and leave me, Allen. You've been talking about it all day. That's what you want to do anyway."

"That's *not* what I want to do," Allen said angrily. "But you have to do your share. Jesus Christ, baby, you can't just bitch about everything. This isn't a camping trip. We're in the middle of a goddamn disaster."

"Go fuck yourself," she mumbled.

"What did you say?" he yelled.

"I said you're an asshole and that you're doing a lousy job of leading us anywhere and that you don't know where you're going and you should let someone else try."

"We're *trying* to get out of the city," he said. Everything has been completely destroyed and people are killing each other in the streets and we're in terrible danger."

"I *know* people are killing each other in the streets." Her voice had risen a pitch. "You don't have to tell me that people are killing each other in the streets. My *child* was just clubbed to death by some lunatic in the middle of the street."

"*My* child, too," he said.

She started to scream and curse at him. She called him a lame dick and an emotional cripple.

"Don't get hysterical," he said. His voice sounded on the edge of breaking. "It's not going to help if you freak out. We need all the strength we have."

"You sound like a boy scout leader," she yelled. "Who says I shouldn't freak out? Why *not* freak out? We all might have a better chance if we freaked out instead of creeping around trying to figure out some half assed plan. It's all *over*, don't you understand that?"

An older woman's voice interrupted.

"Why don't you both be quiet? Anyone hiding in this block has been able to hear you. For god's sake, remember what happened to Andrew."

"She's right," another man said. "We got to keep it together until we find a place to spend the night. It's going to get worse when it gets dark."

"We can try that restaurant across the street," the older woman said.

"No, I don't think that would be a good idea," Allen said.

"Oh, you don't," said his wife. "And just where should we eat?"

"Why don't you stop bugging me?" he shouted. "In fact, why don't you get out of my life?"

"I was just going," she said.

"No, I'll go," he said.

"OK, you go."

He walked away.

"Chunka chunka chunka," someone said. Then he made other, less intelligible sounds.

"Wheeeeee," a voice shouted.

"Let him go," a man said. "He wasn't doing anyone any good."

There was a short hollow gasp followed by a long groan.

"Stop him," a woman screamed.

"Stop who?"

"Mr. Riggins. He's mutilating himself."

"Don't look."

"It seems like a hundred years ago that we were at that camp site in Oregon, doesn't it, Pauline?"

"We're paying for the sins of a hundred years."

"At least that. Five hundred years."

"Call it two hundred. You always exaggerate."

"Let's get into that restaurant."

"Heh heh heh."

"What?"

I had lost track of the voices.

"You just want me to tell you where to go, well, smart ass, I don't know where to go."

"I know you don't know where to go."

"Come on, don't lean on me all the time. I can't carry your weight when you do that to me."

"It wasn't me that killed those two this morning. I would never have done it."

"We're here, aren't we?"

129

"We'll have to talk about what happened sometime."

"I hate it when you say that. Talk about what? What are we going to talk about?"

"Nothing. About what happened."

They walked away. I lay still until I couldn't hear them anymore. The I took off the hub cap and sat up. I saw the last one disappear through the window of the restaurant. A man lay slumped against a Coke machine that stood upended in the middle of the street. He wore tennis shorts and a fork was sticking out of his bare chest. I walked down the middle of the street. Men stood silhouetted on roofs but I didn't care. They could maim me or do whatever they wanted or I could slash into them. I was ready either way. A helicopter skimmed over the buildings behind me and I hobbled and fell into a doorway. Men called to each other. The shouts grew closer and then stopped. My body refused to move out into the street. It was getting dark. The buildings across the street had fallen into deep shadows while my side was still in the light. "Wa wa wa wa wa wa," I howled, and then again. The sounds frightened me. They seemed to approach hunting sounds although they were still timid, still restricted to the throat.

A large bearded man in a blue and gold football helmet and red terry cloth bathrobe walked down the middle of the street, dragging one leg and singing softly to himself. He used a baseball bat for a cane, stopping every few steps to swing it around his head or tap it on the ground. His head swung wildly around until his eyes focused on me. He sank to his knees, laying his bat in front of him and bending his head, as if in prayer. I stepped into the door of a toy store, picking my way through the smashed toys and discarding a spear gun and bicycle pump in favor of a croquet mallet. Five men had gathered behind him. They shouted encouragement as he limped forward. He stopped to level the bat a few times across his chest as if he was preparing to swing at a ball. Then he came on. Down the street a dog barked and then howled as other dogs joined in. I stepped further back, hiding behind hanging bicycle tire and nylon warm up jackets. I picked up a croquet ball, shifting the mallet underneath my other arm. As he came through the door I threw the croquet ball and then grabbed the mallet with my good hand. The ball struck him on the shoulder but he still came on, a guttural clucking sound coming from deep in his throat. I clucked back at him and he stopped. I wanted to say something that would at least make him hesitate, to let him know that I meant him no harm, except that I wanted to kill him. "How are ya doin?" I asked. I was unable to say anything more and he stepped up to me. He had a broad gentle face with a small mustache on his upper lip. He swung the bat and smashed a row of games and fishing tackle off a shelf. He swung the bat at a

131

higher shelf. Small rubber and plastic balls bounced around our feet. I slid along the wall, trying to squeeze past him towards the door. He dropped the bat and sprang towards me, pressing me with his huge chest into a corner, I swung the mallet but it bounced off his helmet. He casually knocked the mallet out of my hand and I grabbed him around the chest and kissed him on the throat. He gurgled and spat at me. His huge arms encircled me in a suffocating hug and we whirled around the store, smashing through toys and tipping over the shelves. We stopped, breathless. "God laughs at me," he whispered into my ear. "But his laughter is my love." Then he threw me to the ground and held me down with one boot while he reached up for the bicycle tires that hung above him on a rack. He held eight of them on one arm and shoved them over me as he forced me to stand up. Then he knocked me down again and rolled me through the wreckage. He waited while I crawled out of the tires and then he half lifted, half dragged me out the door and deposited me on the street. He kicked me methodically in the stomach and back and I had to protect my groin by curling into myself and screaming, as if I had already been damaged there. He walked around me, grunting and kicking. He spat on me and stepped away. I lay with my eyes closed while the other men gathered around me.

"I don't figure there's much sense in stompin him to death," said a soft southern voice. "He don't look like the one we was after anyway."

"We could cut off his head and put it up on one of them sticks," said another voice.

"Well, I don't know," said the southern voice. "That would be attracting a lot of attention."

I opened my eyes. The voice belonged to a thin man in white cotton pants and a black Nehru shirt. Gray hair fell over his forehead and his narrow eyes squinted down at me as if he had trouble seeing that far.

"It's one hell of a mysterious day," he said dreamily.

I wasn't able to reply.

"Well, now, this is the way I see it," he said, as if I had asked him a question. "The city has broken into little pathological groups. Ours has been in the making for some time now so we're a little better prepared than the others. You might say that this day has given expression to what has always been latent within us. But I *am* sorry that we made a mistake with you."

He looked away and when he looked back he had tears in his eyes.

"We knew it would come but never like this. I feel bone crushing good but it won't last. The remorse, god, the remorse."

He kicked me swiftly in the side of my head, then stepped away, looking down at me with his hands on his hips.

"*You* say something," he said. "You try and

make sense out of why we've degenerated into street scum. How it's all tipped over on us. I can't wait on things anymore."

He turned his back. Two men squatted beside my head. One was the bearded man in the helmet, the other a small stocky man with a misshapen saturnine face that had an ear missing. He wore black Indian moccasins and a red and white blanket draped over his shoulders. The bearded man sighed and clucked his tongue at me. The other man pursed his lips, trying to whistle, only no sound came out. He opened and shut his mouth several times showing me proudly that half his tongue had been cut off. I shut my eyes and then opened them again. They were still squatting before me. The other men had made a pile out of furniture and boxes. One of them dribbled gasoline from a plastic container over the pile and lit a match to it. The wood burst into flames and they soon had hamburgers cooking on a grill and hot dogs and marshmallows roasting on the ends of fiber glass fishing rods. A case of whisky was smashed open and a bottle passed around. The man with the black Nehru shirt walked slowly around the fire, drinking from a bottle and kicking at anyone near him. The bearded man and the man with the missing ear walked over to the fire. The bearded man returned, carrying two burnt marshmallows between the thumb and forefinger of each hand. "Oh, I feel so beautiful," he said. "The pain has gone from my

134

neck into my solar plexus." He rolled me over on my back with his foot and placed the marshmallows firmly over my eyes. The marshmallows were still hot and they stuck to my eyelids. They kept me from weeping and the blood and broken teeth kept me from crying out. The man with the southern voice talked to someone nearby:

"You and I have a date, honey. No shuckin me this time. I'm not all that passive. Nossir, I didn't bring all this down but now that it's down I aim to stay with it."

He moved to the other side of the fire. Feet shuffled up to me. Catsup and mustard were spread over my body and into my hair. Whisky was poured over my face and down to my crotch. I was tickled and prodded. I felt a weight on my stomach and I tried to sit up but I was kicked back to the ground. The object on my stomach fell off but it was roughly shoved back into place. It fell off again and this time it was strapped across me with a belt that was drawn so tight that it threatened my breathing. Sticks and metal rods were banged on the hood of a car. A man moaned and then two or three of them sang "Silver Threads Among the Gold" very slowly. The singing was drowned out by the whir of a helicopter. The helicopter came in low over the street and I felt the wind from the propeller blades and a spark from the scattered fire. It made another pass and then disappeared. I could hear them gathering up blankets and equipment. I raised up

135

on one elbow and slowly pulled a marshmallow
from one eye but part of it stuck to my eyelid and it
was several minutes before I could actually see. A
severed head had been placed on my stomach. I
pushed the head through the belt and rolled away
from it. I tried to make a sound but was unable to
produce more than a grunt. The inside of my ears
roared and I was unable to move, even to remove
the other marshmallow. I was jerked to my feet and
a towel was thrown over my head and twisted
around my neck. A rope was tied around my waist
and I was pulled forward. I felt only pain and yet
somehow I moved, afraid to fall, afraid to even
hesitate. We stopped and I was allowed to rest
although the towel remained over my head. I
listened to the man with the southern voice:

"They'll rebuild all this and we won't
remember it happened. That's the way of this
country. Thank god, my dear, that we can't
remember who we are, what we've come from. But
it does give us a little pocket of depraved time to
stretch out in. I wouldn't abuse it if I were you. It
might never come again. This is where the garage
used to be. We'll rebuild that. The pool still stands.
Oh honey luscious, but we had some wild ex-
travaganzas by that little piss hole of chlorined
water. Martha must have pleasured a thousand
people on this veranda. Not just your usual trash,
either. We figured to take it all, sugar; politics,
show business, the whole creamy meringue."

A dog sniffed at my head and worked his way

down my body. He licked vaguely at the catsup and mustard, prodding into my balls before he padded away.

"We got to move," said a shrill voice. "Fires have broken out in the valley and the whole eastern section is closed off."

"Who *is* this man?" asked the southern voice. He gently prodded my leg with the toe of his shoe.

"He wandered in after the Sierra Alta raid," said another voice.

"We'll skirt the valley," said the southern voice. "We'll regroup at the lake. It's longer that way but we've got food and equipment up there."

I was jerked to my feet and we moved on. We crossed a lawn and then a street and another lawn. We had walked for about half an hour when a man was shot in front of me. He fell backwards, knocking me over as well. He must have been shot very cleanly because he didn't move. There was a shot fired from our group and then no one moved for a long time. Two men whispered next to me:

"Who the fuck are they?"

"Who knows? But they got us pinned. There might not be more than a dozen of them but they got the street blocked."

"What about those buildings over there? We could go through them and come out the other side."

"Too risky. I can't think. All these fucking strategies."

"We got to draw their fire in some way and

137

we'll get through that gate over yonder and go around them."

"We'll send the guy in the towel."

"You mean that creep over there?"

"Yeah, the guy they been sportin on."

"Well, shit, hustle him on up there."

A knife jabbed me in the thigh. I stood up. A pistol was put into my hand and I was turned around and pointed in a direction. I pulled the trigger but the pistol was empty. Another bullet whined off to the side and I sank to my knees. A knife prodded into the small of my back and I stood up again and tried a few steps. Nothing happened. I walked forward. Suddenly they were no longer behind me. I whirled around, chopping at the air with the gun butt. I ran a few steps and then stumbled and fell over the rope dragging behind me. I stood up and someone slashed into the rope with a knife. I tried to reach out for him but he stepped off to the side. I shivered, as if coming apart. I moaned for help. Then the gun was taken from my hand and I was led by one finger to a bench. I sat, trying to listen to the voices around me.

"Leave the towel over him. He's probably better off that way."

"That bunch was crazy. I think they had some kind of religion the way they charged around and then ran like hell."

"It'll be quiet now. There will be sort of an obscene lull before night sets in."

"Thank god I no longer dream no more. I'm afraid to think on the kinks I seen today."

I moaned: "Unnnnnnnnnhhhhhhh."

"He's done for. I'm going back in. I don't care if it is like some kind of weird church in there. I seen enough pain."

I slumped back on the bench. The towel was removed from my head. I blinked, trying to see. The figure who had removed the towel was walking away, into the middle of a huge warehouse or factory. The light had nearly faded but I could distinguish tin corrugated walls. Most of the roof had fallen in and in front of me were hundreds of wooden crates and rows of white enamel bathtubs and toilets. Machine parts, huge airplane engines and loose coils of manila rope had been piled up near the walls. Near the entrance several Ping-Pong tables had been arranged where Red Cross women served cold coffee and candy bars. Naked figures lay in the bathtubs and sat on the toilets, while heads stared over the edges of the crates. As I stepped further inside I was conscious of hundreds of small coos and sighs.

"I'm glad you found us," said one of the Red Cross women. She smoothed back her blue tinted hair and handed me a paper cup of coffee and a Clark bar. She wore a starched gray uniform and carried her left arm in an impeccable white sling. "We have gathered here until things get sorted out. It shouldn't be too long. One of the ladies will get your information later on." She tried to whistle.

139

"God respects me when I work," she said, trying for a smile, "but he loves me when I sing."

I stepped past her. A wrinkled white haired man pulled at my sleeve. He lay in a bathtub with his neck hanging over the edge, his feet on the faucets. His voice was low and insistent:

"Midway was a beautiful naval exercise. The Coral Sea was good but Midway was better. I was there. I spent the whole time below decks with a sunburn. Listen, throw some water on me. If there was water in here I could remember thirty more battles. I'm wonderful on Trafalgar and Pearl Harbor."

I sat down on a toilet. A woman on the toilet next to mine offered me a cigarette. I placed it mechanically between my lips. She was very stout and wore yellow curlers in her hair. "I'm not going to light it for you," she said. She looked at me hard, her shoulders shivering with disdain. "I don't care what kind of day you had. I'm no masochist."

She stood up and walked to a crate behind her. The crate was five feet wide and just as high. She knocked on the wood with her knuckles and cried out for Jacob. She knocked again and kicked a few times. Then she came back and sat down on the toilet.

"I know he's in there," she said. "The little worm. I'm scared. There's a fire back there and I've always had a fear of fires. When I was a kid our garage burned to the ground. I'm not good on birds either but that's no problem now, is it? I mean, there aren't any bats flying around that I can see."

I looked behind her. Near the far wall several thin layers of smoke drifted up towards the ceiling.

She began to cry. "I knew he would leave me when it got tough. What's that thing the football coaches say: 'That's when the tough get going.' Well, he never had the balls. Sarah, that's my youngest sister, has got him off somewhere. I'm so ashamed. But I know where. In that crate, that's where. C'mon, I'm gonna ask a favor of you, and you a stranger, too. But this is no time for manners, right?"

She stood up and walked back to the crate.

"I'm alone here, Jacob," she yelled. "Jacob, I said I'm afraid to go through this alone. I'm going crazy. I'm liable to do anything. Oooooooooooo," she moaned. "Did you hear that? You're going to pay, Jacob. You're going to pay very heavily, and it's going to hurt too."

She turned to me and kissed me on the cheek. She licked some mustard off my shoulders and ran her hands down my chest. She motioned for me to kneel and I knelt down and she stepped up on my back, hoisting herself over the edge. I tried to climb in after her but I couldn't make it. The flames had grown higher and clouds of smoke drifted through the opening. in the roof.

Her head appeared over the edge of the crate. "Mister," she cried. "He's dead, mister. What am I going to do now?"

I walked away.

I heard humming coming from a crate nearby and I walked over to it. Aluminum wheelbarrows were piled up behind the crate and I wheeled one over to the side. The humming changed into long sobbing chants. "Mooooooooo," cried a male voice and then was joined by two female voices. I stood on the wheelbarrow and peered over the edge. A man and woman sat against one side, their arms around each other. A plump golden haired girl lay across their laps. The man was bleeding from the chest and shoulders. The woman was holding a wrist up in the air which she had just slashed with a piece of tin. Blood dripped through her flabby breasts onto the round stomach of the girl. The man and woman had pressed their cheeks together, as if forming one face. They both wore wedding rings and all three wore silver identification bracelets. They looked up at me, singing out: "Nooooooo. No. No. No. Oh, who do you think you are, think you are, think you are, oh, who do you think you are, so early in the morning?" They scowled up at me, their eyes pleading at me to come in. They sang again: "Oh no, you can't come in, can't come innnnnnnnn." I pulled one leg over the edge but I couldn't manage to lift the other one. The girl stood up and pulled me over. I sat opposite them, unable to move. The three of them were crouching in one corner. The man passed out, his head falling on the woman's lap. The woman shoved her bleeding wrist under her armpit, as if she wanted to stop the flow of blood. I took off my shirt and threw it at her but she let it fall at her feet. The girl crawled over to the other corner on my side of the crate.

"I've never seen them before," she whispered. "They were singing so I thought they had something going. I thought they knew what to do. As soon as I climbed in they started slashing themselves up."

"Don't listen to the little pervert," the woman said. "She happens to be our only daughter. She led us here with her groovy far-out friends. She said they were the only ones who would let us through. She said they had prepared for this apocalypse for a long time. My husband and I own a dog kennel and real estate in San Diego. You haven't heard about San Diego, have you?"

I shook my head. Her husband glanced wildly around. "I'm prepared," he said. "Let no man or group of men say that I'm not prepared."

His head slumped back to his wife's lap.

"We're prepared, all right," his wife said. "We're prepared like a whale in the desert. We'll go out in this box. It's like a coffin."

She picked up the shirt and wrapped it tightly around her wrist.

"It's too late," the daughter said.

"I know it's too late," the mother replied. She moved over to the free corner on her side of the crate. Now all the corners were full.

"They can't get out," the daughter said to me.

"They're too weak. But as soon as they fade, I'm off. Aren't I, Mama?"

"Yes, you are, dear," the mother sighed. "You'll climb right over us and rush out into that friendly world of yours."

They stared at each other and then they burst into tears. The girl rushed to her mother and buried her head in her lap. The mother stroked her daughter's hair.

"We can get out, Mama," the daughter said.

"Maybe we can. My wrist isn't cut too deeply."

"Everything will be all right, won't it?" the daughter asked.

"Yes, baby," the mother said. "Everything is going to be fine. This will all blow over. There will be green grass where all the filth is now and German shepherds romping over everything. We'll be better off from what happened. We won't make the same mistakes next time."

The father raised his head.

"We're not licked yet," he said.

The light from the flames had begun to dance over the edge of the crate. It was getting very hot. The girl went back to her corner. She stared at me with large vacant eyes. Fists pounded on the wall.

"You're gonna burn in there," a voice yelled.

"We're getting out," the daughter said.

"Nonsense," her mother said. "We're safe in here. We don't know those people out there. We're together now and no one can surprise us."

The daughter stood up and screamed: "There's a fire. I can smell it. There are flames over there."

"Sit down, dear," her father said. "There have been fires all day. One more isn't going to make any difference."

I stood up and looked over the edge. The flames covered the entire rear of the warehouse and several crates were beginning to go up. Most of the bathtubs and toilets were empty although there were a few who had decided to sit it out. They sat with their arms wrapped around themselves or each other, rocking back and forth. Screams and yells came from inside several crates. I turned and faced the inside of my own crate. They were still crouched in their separate corners. The girl had drawn her legs up to her chest. She was crying. Her mother was staring reproachfully at her and her father had picked up a thin piece of tin and was slicing it over the length of his arms and legs. I stepped over to the girl and stamped and pounded my head on the wall but she chose to look at the floor. I made a leap for the wall but wasn't able to climb over. I tried again, stepping on the girl's shoulder. She bit me on the leg. I stepped on her head and pulled myself over the edge. I hung for a moment, unable to go either way, and then I fell over. I lay on the ground. I could hear them singing but I couldn't distinguish the words. A woman ran by, her hair on fire. I hobbled behind an old man in a white skullcap pushing an aluminum wheelbarrow. Another old man, his neck covered by a blue silk scarf, sat cross-legged in the wheelbarrow and urged him on.

"Hurry up, you useless prick," he yelled. "We'll be burned alive in here."

"I'm doing fifty more steps and then you take over," said the man in the skullcap. "One, two, three, four, five, six, seven, eight . . ."

"When you finally get something worth pushing you can't do it," yelled the one in the scarf.

"I'm dumping you," said the one with the skullcap. "Ten more steps and then you're carrying me."

"Twenty more steps," the other one said. "And then you can dump me in the fire. I don't give a fuck. It's better than having to look at you."

The one with the skullcap stopped pushing the wheelbarrow and I caught up with them. They stared at each other, their eyes bright with hate. They were both short and emaciated and neither of them had hair on their bodies.

"The old pumper, eh?" shouted the one with the scarf. "Five more minutes if you're lucky and then it's ashes for you."

"Your turn," said the one with the skullcap. He sat down wheezing and rubbing his heart. "We'll see how long you last with those ninety pounds of bullshit you're made of."

The one with the scarf climbed out and I climbed in. I pressed my hands together as if in prayer. They conferred together in whispers.

"Twenty steps apiece," said the one with the scarf. "You're one, he's two and I'm three. In that order. When we get free it's every man for himself."

They both got in the wheelbarrow and I picked up the handles and hobbled forward a few feet. Behind us the flames rose in a burning wall.

"Fourteen more steps," shouted the one with the scarf. "Move it. Move it. Get your thumb out of your ass."

"Hee haw, hee haw, hee haw," shouted the other one.

I did twenty steps and stopped. The one with the scarf replaced me. I fell back on the one with the skullcap.

"Don't get too close," he said angrily. "I don't like it when people get too close." His breath was foul and his body that of a skeleton. "On," he cried. "On, you broken match sticks. Hurry! Hurry! Hurry!"

We were pushed a few feet and then the one with the scarf stopped, almost tipping us over. His eyes were bulging and a vein above his right eye seemed about to burst.

"He can't make it," shouted the one with the skullcap. He pounded my back. "You see that. He's going to die on us. Go ahead. Die. Do it. Do it."

We were pushed another few feet and we stopped again.

"Unnnnnhhhhhh," moaned the one with the scarf. He pushed us the final steps and collapsed.

147

He gasped for breath and looked at the one with the skullcap who had shrunk behind me.

"Now, you toothless cocksucker," he wheezed. "Your turn. Only you'll go under after ten steps. Come on, get out. You haven't been outside the warehouse in five years. Living like a mole in there. You'll die now. And it won't be from sunlight."

The one with the skullcap crawled out of the wheelbarrow and took his place between the handles. The one with the scarf got in beside me, pushing me back so that he could see in front of him. We had managed to leave the warehouse and were facing a large parking lot near a destroyed shopping center.

"All right," said the one with the scarf. "Haul ass. You've left your home and all that's in it. You won't last more than a day out of your crate. No talking to yourself out here. No staring for six months and sucking each finger. That don't go out here."

We were pushed a few feet and then the one with the skullcap sank down between the handles. He kneeled on the ground and leaned his chin over the edge of the wheelbarrow.

"No more," he sighed.

We lay without moving as the flames rose straight up into the sky behind us and naked figures ran past. There was no sound from the one with the skullcap. He had sagged to the ground and lay on his back, his arms thrown out to the sides.

148

"He's dead," said the one with the scarf. "I outlasted him. And I even got a few more breaths. But I outlasted him, didn't I? Eh? I knew he was going. I saw it this morning when he ran around screaming and banging on the crates. The roof almost fell in on top of him. He stood there and let it fall and I got to give him that. We hadn't heard a word from him in over a year and his crate was right in the middle of the goddamn warehouse. Then he starts talking. He starts going on about the mountains and little streams running through the hills and delicatessens he knew where he could catch fish and flowers. I believe he yelled out the names of flowers and pickles and television programs he used to like. He was going then. We all knew it but he was sparking, he was, all day he was walking up and down sparking like crazy. Yeah, but he's dead now, isn't he? Eh?"

I climbed out of the wheelbarrow and the one with the scarf fell off to the side. He didn't look at his companion. He made himself as small as possible, tucking his withered head into the bony hollow of his shoulder and folding his legs up into his chest.

"We're on cement, ain't we?" he asked. "I can't see too good. Give me some sign that we might be on some grass."

I grunted.

"Now give me some sign that I'm not going to roast lying here."

I tapped him on the leg with my foot.

"Now give me some sign that we got through this day and that everything is going to be all right."

I tapped him again.

"Now put the wheelbarrow over me and go away."

I tipped the wheelbarrow over him so that only a foot and one hand were visible. I crossed a street and turned down another one, trying to put several buildings between myself and the flames. It was very dark and I needed to move, to try and move, to one more place. I passed a burning supermarket. Four figures ran through the flames carrying hams and steaks and bottles of liquor. Two small girls waited outside near shopping carts piled high with food. "Unnnnnnnnnnhhhhhhh, " the sound came out unbidden. I walked through an empty lot, then past a blasted laundromat, my feet dragging through shirts and pants. "Unnnnnnnnhhhhhh," the sound came out again. I stood in the ruins of a department store. Furniture, bedding, games, lingerie, lamps, television sets, gourmet goods, china, silverware, perfumes were strewn everywhere. I had no idea how to pick anything up. I followed a man in a white plastic raincoat. He pushed a shopping cart full of bricks, walking fast, not looking to the right or left. I followed him down a driveway and then across a rough patch of ground covered with high bushes and high grass. He had trouble pushing the shopping cart and several times he had to get in front of it and pull. I kept twenty feet behind him, trying to stay in the shadows. We crossed several intersections and finally turned down a long narrow street. It was very dark except for a small fire several blocks away. I became aware of other figures moving down the street, carrying bricks, milk crates and pieces of wood. The man in the raincoat disappeared among them as they dropped their loads on the other side of the fire. A rough wall or barricade was forming across the width of the street. Naked men and women worked on top of the low wall, piling up the objects that were handed to them. On the other side of the wall I could make out the dim outlines of one story buildings. I sat down. An old man in gray corduroy pants and a red nylon hunting cap stared into the fire.

"You're the last one," he said. "We don't have no room for no more refugees or them that lays about dying."

He didn't blink his eyes and as I looked closer I saw that he was blind.

"It's a boneyard all around," he said. "They got to close the street. They don't close the street and they'll get overrun. You got anything to eat?"

He didn't wait for an answer but mumbled to himself and lay down on his side. Then he sat upright, his head wobbling back and forth.

"No, you won't do," he said. "Not enough noise in you. They're only taking those that make noise. I heard them talking. I don't pay them no

151

mind. They didn't ask me but I'll be damned if I'll go anyway."

Instead of making me drowsy, the fire caused me to weep and I dug my fingers into my thigh.

"Aaaaaaargh," I cried.

"What's that?" the old man said. His head was directed towards me. "How many of you are there? Room for one more, that's all."

The man in the raincoat stood near the fire, thrusting out his hands as if they needed warmth.

"We can fill in the holes later with mud and cement," he said. "After that the wire goes on top and no one gets in. I'm telling you now so you'll know you've been told. But there's no . . . Hmmmmmmm . . . no sense thinking you'll be let in without helping . . . Hmmmmmmmm . . ."

His voice had broken into a low hum. He took off his raincoat and let it drop to his feet. He was very thin.

"I'm leaving this here," he said. "You can wrap it around the old man."

He walked down the street, away from the wall and the fire.

"I've heard him before," said the blind man. "Hell, you're not the first one he's said that to. Don't get excited or nothing. They been doing this all afternoon. Why don't you say something? You trying to move in on me or something? I got nothing you want."

A knife appeared in his right hand and he

slashed around him. He stopped after a while and lay down again on his side. I crawled over to the wall. I sat a few feet away and watched them build it. They were using as many bricks, cinder blocks and rocks as possible. They had even managed to include a smashed car. A large woman moved past me and heaved two suitcases onto the wall. She stepped on my ankle and whirled around to face me.

"You'll have to move off," she said. "We can't let you get too close. We've been attacked twice in the last few hours. We, aaaahhhh, well, we, ooooooh, we'll be finishing up soon and then this whole part of the street will be blocked off."

"Unnnnnnnnnnhhhh," I said.

She sat down and smoothed out the dirt in front of her.

"It's been awful," she said. Her broad face was heightened by black penciled eyebrows. "But we can't help you. We can only take those that are able. I can see that you've been smashed up pretty bad."

I nodded.

Her lips circled together and her eyes closed. "Oooooooooooo," she wailed.

She looked at me and shook her head.

"I'm just resting. I'm not giving you any sympathy. We have enough food for a month. Arms as well. No one will get to us. . . . We'll have time to wait out a plague. . . . Oh god, I should be working. I shouldn't be talking like this."

She stood up and climbed on top of the wall and shouted for someone to hand her something.

"Ahhhhhhh," the sound came out of me. I walked up to the wall and tried to climb up. I stepped on some old flower pots that gave way beneath me. I fell, landing on my back. Two men picked me up underneath my arms and dragged me back to the fire

"Don't try it again," one of them said after I was dropped to the ground. "We'll shoot you if you get too close again."

He sank to his knees, his head hanging between his legs.

"Don't make an attempt," he said. "Don't get . . . uuuuooooh . . . I can't move. I won't be able to get back. They'll never take me."

His companion looked at him and then walked away, towards the wall.

"Try," I was able to mumble. "We'll both go. But ahhh . . ."

I wasn't able to continue. He lay down next to the blind man. I put the raincoat over him.

"It's more open out here," said the blind man. "You don't want to get close to them. They got it all organized, all set up. No telling what might happen out here. Better that way."

He mumbled to himself and laughed a few times. A flashlight flickered over the wall. It was getting higher.

"Unnnhhhh," I moaned.

I hobbled away from the fire, towards the other end of the street. I needed something to add to the wall. A brick might be enough. A bullet split the street in front of me and then there was another shot, the bullet whining off against a car fender. Two or three men ran past dragging a heavy tarpaulin behind them. I walked on. There were small bursts of rifle fire in front of me but my body no longer reacted. I reached a pile of rubble and sat down. "Waaaaaaaahhh," I cried out. I reached forward. I touched a leg and withdrew my hand. I peered over the body, trying to see if it was dead. I crawled around it. "Ump, ump, ump," I grunted. I looked back for the fire. It still glowed down the street. I picked up a brick.

"Wa wa wa wa," a voice mumbled.

I dropped the brick. The voice was very close, a few feet in front of me. I lay down. The figure was lying on his stomach, his arms folded underneath his chin. I picked the brick up again. "Wooooooo," I cried out. "Wooooooooooooo . . ." I raised the brick over my head. He had raised a brick as well.

"Wa wa wa wa wa," he cried. We brought our bricks high over our heads and on the downward arc they struck together. We lay panting, our bricks fallen to the ground. I reached out for him but he picked up his brick and slammed it down on my fingers.

"Aiieeeeee," I cried and I could hear his cry over mine. Then it fell away to a sob. I backed away,

155

keeping my brick and picking up another one. He was striking forward with his, crawling after me. I stood up and drew back my foot to kick him in the face. He lay still. I kicked him anyway and brought the brick down on his head. I sat down and held his smashed head in my arms.

"I have nothing to say," he said. "Don't be afraid. It will happen to you soon enough."

"Waaaaah," I cried out.

"It doesn't matter," he said. His voice was soft and fading fast but his words were very clear.

"I wanted you to do it," he said. "Couldn't get it done myself."

He died, not making a sound. I sat for a while, cradling his head. Then I stood up and walked back towards the fire.

I sat down next to the blind man. The area was crowded and there was now almost a complete circle of people around the fire. Next to me sat a man and a woman. They were young and suntanned and wore expensive camping gear. The woman was unrolling their sleeping bags while the man removed a suede hiking boot and rubbed his foot. The other figures were all men. They sat naked to the waist, passing around a bottle and checking their rifles. I could make out four of them.

"We got one more?" said the blind man. "Well, you're the last one. We'll build up our own goddamn wall."

The wall was two feet higher. There seemed to

156

be more people working on it and I could make out two men sitting on the top with rifles.

"I think that scene is full of lunatics," said the man with the camping gear.

"Aahhhhhhh," I cried. The other men looked up at me and sighed. One of them passed me the bottle and I took a slug. I passed it on.

"Those people," the woman whispered. "I don't want to be too close."

She lay down on the sleeping bag and he lay next to her, holding her and stroking her hair. "It should get better now," she said. "I mean, the worst must be over."

"In a few days you won't even remember most of it," he said. "We'll start all over. But we'll take a vacation first."

There were more flashlights playing over the wall. Occasionally the light would play over us and then dart away. The men cleaning their rifles didn't seem to mind.

"These are bad times," said the blind man. "That's all. Those people on the wall will get what's coming to them."

"Amen," said one of the men.

Two of the men crawled away to the right. After a few minutes another slid away.

"Now you take thirty years ago," said the blind man. "The Philippines. Luzon. Now that was bad. But hell, we joined hands and wiped the sons of bitches clean away."

I crawled off. I still had my brick and I made my way towards the wall. It was the end now for me. I had no more strength. I reached the edge of the wall. Little dribbles of rubble fell from the top. One of the guards peered down at me. I tried to put my brick up near his feet but I didn't have the strength. I could hear moans behind the wall. "Unnnnnnn," I said. The guard raised his rifle and pointed it at me. A bullet struck his foot and he fell off to the side. I slid down to the ground. There was firing all around, bullets striking the wall and the ground. Rifles poked through holes in the wall and fired back. I looked towards the fire but it was no longer there. I crept along the side of the wall. I reached the side of the street and collapsed behind an uprooted tree. I could go no further. The firing had stopped and it was suddenly very quiet. I was afraid, I remember that. "Oooooooooh," I prayed before I passed out. "Oooooooooooh."